1998.6

1998.6 by Matthew Roberson

Normal/Tallahassee

Published by FC2 with support provided by Florida State University, the
Unit for Contemporary Literature of the Department of English at Illinois
State University, the Program for Writers of the Department of English of
the University of Illinois at Chicago, and the Illinois Arts Council.

Address all inquiries to: Fiction Collective Two, Florida State
University, c/o English Department, Tallahassee, FL 32306-1580

ISBN: Paper, 1-57366-102-3

Library of Congress Cataloging-in Publication Data
Roberson, Matthew.
  1998.6 / Matthew Roberson.— 1st ed.
    p. cm.
A rewriting of Ronald Sukenick's novel 98.6.
  ISBN 1-57366-102-3
1. Graduate students—Fiction. 2. Group homes—Fiction.
3. Internet—Fiction. I. Sukenick, Ronald. 98.6. II. Title.
PS3618.O3167 A15 2002
813'.6--dc21
                        2002008404

Cover Design: Victor Mingovits
Book Design: Tara Reeser
Cover Photo: Harry Ransom Humanities Research Center,
The University of Texas at Austin

Produced and printed in the United States of America
Printed on recycled paper with soy ink

This program is
partially supported by
a grant from the
Illinois Arts Council

For Gretchen

Acknowledgments

The work of Gilles Deleuze and Félix Guattari included on pages 124, 240, 249, and 253 comes from *A Thousand Plateaus: Capitalism and Schizophrenia*, Minneapolis: University of Minnesota Press, 1993.

Many thanks to Patrick Sharp, Melissa Watts, Cam Tatham, Lynn Tatham, David Crane, and Ron Sukenick, who were kind enough to let me use their photos here.

Many, many thanks to Ron Sukenick, for not only playing along with this project, but for being a great support. Ralph Berry and Brenda Mills also delivered fantastic advice through the revision and publishing process.

I couldn't have written this book without the generous help of my folks, Herman and Jeannette Roberson.

And Gretchen.... Of course....

Frankenstein

9/12 a shadow solidifies in the mist. The beach perfect
in size and shape a half moon with white white sand. The
sloop tacks struggling into the harbormouth wallowing in
the swell a jagged open wound on its front port side.
Skipper sends them up the bay on a close beat bow bobbing through the chop while he hauls in sail slicker shining.
It's just dawn. They're struggling into the island. Skipper
grounds onto the beach heads up as he drops the main
halyard Skipper handles the jibsheet as they come about.
He topples over the side of the boat lithe like a monkey
one arm clutching the rail. His body extends far enough so
he can drop. Skipper throws the anchor his way he pulls it
far up along the beach.

Welcome to your island says Skipper your feet hit it
first I'll get the others from below throws him an emergency
kit.

What's this for he says.

For emergencies Skipper says annoyed his eyes
rolling.

What emergencies he says.

I don't know what emergencies Skipper says his arms
flying up you'll know them when you see them he thinks
of another question not a good one but a question enough
to create a dialogue. He doesn't ask it it isn't the time. How
does he know you ask. You intuit. That's how you do it.

5/16 The Wife's going to cancel cable they only watch a couple hours a night she says and it's the free stuff. She bends over her checkbook paying bills. It's Sunday. The evening is warm and muggy. The Wife's said a dozen times she's going to cancel cable The Wife hasn't canceled cable. Working all day on the weekdays she doesn't have time to call the cable company arrange an appointment be at home for the (un)installer's visit a weekend cancellation is out of the question. If anyone is going to arrange a cancellation it's going to be him when The Wife says she's going to cancel cable he nods in agreement he doesn't agree really.

Have some iced tea. It's got ginger in it.

It's fifty dollars a month for something we don't use she tears out a finished check slowly a few paper teeth at a time he's in the kitchen but still he hears it.

He sets the iced tea next to her lays his hands on her shoulders. He presses down working his fingers into her muscles. Fifty dollars is ridiculous he says let's cancel it. I'll call tomorrow morning.

Good she says she relaxes she leans into him. Lets out a breath she's been expecting an argument not a passionate defense of the value of cable more an insinuation that they do watch cable more than she's implied a reminder that movies on HBO are cheaper than movies at

the theater a mention of Lifetime Television for Women.
The Wife had been expecting an argument she would
have had answers. He's done the right thing agreeing but
he's not going to cancel cable. He's going to forget his
promise if the issue is pressed he'll fabricate (un)install-
ation meetings that are for one reason or another canceled
forgotten missed. He's not a sneaky person this is not
sneakiness it's just part of a plot. Isn't it.·He's seen it done
in comedies especially it happens always in farces everything from Three's Company to Frasier harmless scheming
one character against the other it's only a matter of some
small desire misdeed misbehavior pursued in secret it
always gets found out resolved a happy ending ha ha. But
not before the one character gets his way over another at
least for a while. No big deal. Is it. He doesn't feel well he
knows life isn't like tv he's a grown man he's not so
stupid. Then again it's all just fiction tv life so why can't
the one be like the other. Maybe he's too smart maybe he
can talk himself into anything. It doesn't matter. The topic
of cancelling tv won't come up again at least not for a
while if it does he'll figure something out he'll have to
because he doesn't watch just a couple of hours of tv a
night he watches a lot more than that he can't do without
The Flintstones Mary Tyler Moore The Bob Newhart Show
The Partridge Family The Monkees St. Elsewhere The
Brady Bunch L.A. Law thirtysomething Talk Soup Magnum
P.I. Hawaii Five-O Win Ben Stein's Money South Park The
Tick The Kids in the Hall Battlestar Galactica Northern
Exposure The Six Million Dollar Man Bonanza Gilligan's
Island.

10/25 his second copy of *98.6* he picked up during
the last hour last day of the annual campus book sale
books were going for a dollar a bag tables were thinning
only a few scattered books spread across the literature
section. It has R. Dent Finch stamped across the title page.
It pleases him that Finch whom he's never liked has given
away donated to the sale his copy of the book it somehow no longer suiting his tastes no longer seeming appropriate in the custom designed custom built bookshelves in
the custom designed custom built suburban home. Maybe
Finch waffled as he held it over his shopping bag of
donations justifying to himself why it wasn't worth keeping too marginal too experimental too much a piece of
outdated nineteen-seventies postmodern white male angst.
Whatever. It doesn't matter now. Finch put it in the bag
and he stumbled across it on a Friday afternoon in spring
the very same week he was teaching the very same book
in his upper-level survey of contemporary fiction and now
it's his. He didn't want a bag of books for a dollar on that
last hour of the last day of the annual library book sale
upstairs in an enormous meeting room on the fourth floor
of the library people wandering around stuffing random
choices into their flimsy plastic bags. He just wanted that
newold copy of *98.6* he wants everything anything
Sukenick every book he's written and more. Multiple

copies when multiples are available he searches for them on the internet. He has a half dozen copies of *98.6*. He's got first editions galleys he arranges to do reviews of recent stuff gets uncorrected page proofs ahead of publication. He's got pictures of Ron photos photocopied off dust jackets from *The New York Times Book Review*. In his desk at school he keeps a small stack of cards that once fit into the pockets of library copies of Sukenick's books checkout slips three by five cards with author's name and title and call number in real typewriter print. When he's at libraries he always checks for Sukenick books checks for these cards pulls them out puts them in his pocket they're not used anymore anyway everything's barcoded. He even owns a copy of Hollander's film of *Out* it stars of all people a young Peter Coyote a young Danny Glover it wasn't easy to get. It's all for his dissertation he's writing a dissertation on Ronald Sukenick. Right. He doesn't need an entire collection to write a dissertation. He has all he has because he can't write a dissertation. How does that work if you can't pin your subject down in one way you pin him it down another way it's fetishistic. He doesn't like to think about this doesn't like to think he's pathological. So what. He can't imagine not doing what he's doing but. While workers at the front table took a payment heads turned he slipped Finch's *98.6* into the pocket of his green jacket walked out. A woman crouched over a box of books partly slid under the table saw him wrinkled her face.

SUKENICK, Ronald 1932-[1]

Genre:
- Novels
- Short Stories
- Literary criticism and history

Personal Information: Born July 14, 1932, in   ; son of Louis (a dentist) and Ceceile (Frey) Sukenick upper middle-class?; Married Lynn Luria, March 19, 1961 (divorced, 1984).

Nationality:

Education: B.A., 1955; M.A., 1957, Ph.D., 1962.

Addresses: Home: 1505 Bluebell Ave. **Office:** Department of English, Box 226. **Agent:** Ellen Levine Literary Agency, Suite 1205, 432 Park Ave.

Career: Instructor, 1956-58, 1959-61; Instructor, 1961-62; toured   , wrote, and taught in various schools, 1962-66; Assistant professor of English, 1966-67; Assistant professor of English and writing, 1968-69; writer in residence, 1969, and University of   , 1970-72; Professor of English, 1975—, director of creative writing, 1975-77, director of Publications Center, 1986—, founder of exchange program and first exchange professor to

Butler Chair,   , soring, 1981. Publisher,   <u>Book Review</u>, 1977, and   <u>Ice</u>, 1989—. Member of   advisory committee, 1987-90.

Membership(s): PEN, Authors Guild, Authors League of   , National Book Critics Circle, Coordinating Council of Literary Magazines (chairman of board of directors, 1975-77), Collective (founding member).

Awards/Honors: Fulbright fellowships, 1958 and 1984; Guggenheim Foundation fellowship, 1976; National Endowment for the Arts Fellowships, 1980 and 1989; CCLM Award for Editorial Excellence, 1985; Western Book Award for publishing, 1985;   Book Award, Before Columbus Foundation, 1988, for <u>Down and In</u>.

---

[1] Contemporary Authors. GaleNet Databases. Gale Research Online. http://galenet.gale.com. Copyright 1998.

Writings:

Wallace Stevens: Musing the Obscure, University Press, 1967.
Up (novel), Dial, 1968.
The Death of the Novel, and Other Stories, Dial, 1969.
Out (novel), Swallow Press, 1973.
(Contributor) Ray Federman, editor, Surfiction, Swallow
    Press, 1974.
98.6 (novel), Fiction Collective, 1975.
Long Talking Bad Conditions Blues, Fiction Collective, 1979.
In Form, Digressions on the Act of Fiction, Southern
    Illinois University Press, 1985.
The Endless Short Story, Fiction Collective, 1986.
Blown Away (novel), Sun & Moon, 1987.
Down and In: Life in the Underground (nonfiction narrative),
    Beech Tree Books, 1987.
Mosaic Man, FC2, 1999.
Narralogues, SUNY Press, 2000

Contributing editor, The Pushcart Prize Anthology, Pushcart/Avon. Fiction appears in more than ten anthologies published in   and Contributor of fiction to New   Review, Partisan Review, and other periodicals. Contributor of reviews to periodicals, including New   Times Book Review, Partisan Review, and Village Voice. Contributing editor, Fiction International, 1970-84; guest editor, Witness, 1989.

10/01 he has a thing about the extraordinary. He's been told that the extraordinary is an answer to The Problem and he wants to believe in its powers meaning the extension of the ordinary to the point of the incredible. He wants to think that these powers are real that they belong to anyone who isn't blinded by the negative hallucinations of our culture in other words not seeing things that are really there letting the ordinary blot out the extraordinary. Get it. But how to get it the extraordinary sitting home reading watching tv playing on the computer never going wherever outside somewhere else finding the extraordinary making it happen. Maybe it's not out there but in here he thinks. In where in here. Waiting. For what for him. Then what should he do. The best he can is what he figures he makes the most of what's at hand latches onto small things pulls them together mixes them up. Turns twists renovates. In his mind the stories he tells himself about himself. Everything he sees he can surf sample manipulate. He's a recycling machine is what he thinks. Even his ideas of the extraordinary they're other people's ideas he's taken them up taken them over now they're his in a way. As long as they're part of become part of his experience then they're his own original to him. Is this enough is this extraordinary or extraordinarily typical. What's the difference. He doesn't know but it's the best he can do he imagines.

1/21 like every weekday morning five-forty-five the
alarm clock on The Wife's bedside table buzzes she slaps
it once five minutes later a second time five minutes later
a third. She doesn't roll out of bed so much as pivot. Out.
Leaning up on an elbow swinging her legs until she's
sitting and then after that tilting forward standing at first
hunched then not. The Wife doesn't sigh getting out of
bed she groans then moves across the bedroom in the half
darkness until she's got the door open then closed again
behind her. The Wife starts the shower sits on the toilet.
She has hair care products that contain exotic ingredients.
The ABBA Creme Moist shampoo is made from arnica
cherry bark almond calendula lavender. The ABBA Recoup conditioner is made from lavender chamomile mint
juniper. For some days there is Pantene Pro-V Daily
Moisture Renewal Conditioner. For soap she uses green
and orange body gels spreads them over a loofah sponge
scrubs them onto her skin. In the shower The Wife doesn't
think about the day ahead but repeats her routine what
comes next. The Wife steps onto the threadbare blue bath
mat once new from The Boston Store dries off with a gray
towel part of a home products line by Guess. The towel
like the bath mat is worn. It hangs on the back of the
bathroom door. On her teeth The Wife uses dental floss
made by Johnson & Johnson a Woven Fluoride Floss

guaranteed to provide Gentle Gum Care. For brushing she
uses a Mentadent toothbrush angled with a rubber grip on
the handle Mentadent Fluoride Toothpaste With Baking
Soda and Peroxide. Her deodorant is Soft & Dri Silken
Solid it's got a baby powder smell. Though she prefers
panties and bras by Jockey the Naturals line she also
wears panties made by Appel she owns several pairs from
Victoria's Secret. Her mother sometimes buys The Wife
underwear and bras he's not sure why he suspects that
The Wife's mother just needs to buy even when she
herself no longer needs or can find space for one more
thing. To tell maybe a story through things. They speak
after all. What they say exactly has never been clear to
him. But he knows there must be nuances. Of course it's
more than the mother speaking it's the daughter The Wife
telling her own story. Or is she just buying one she's seen
who knows where. He does. On other people in ads on
tv. How much of The Wife's story is her own. How much
is anyone's. He's just like The Wife her mother except his
stories cost less. True or not. While he lies in bed The
Wife returns to the bedroom switches on a lamp in the
corner. She gets dressed: panties bra socks blouse pants or
skirt. If she hasn't decided the night before what to wear
she rustles through her dresser the closet the drawers. She
prefers on some days to wear a slim gold necklace he
purchased for her at Lise & Kato's. She always wears her
wedding ring. Ready to leave she pauses at the door says
I'm leaving. His responses range in kind are similar in
theme Have a good day Drive Carefully I'll miss you.
Downstairs through the living room into the kitchen the
refrigerator opens and shuts as she collects the lunch he's
made for her unless it's a day she'll be going out for
lunch. The garage door rattles the Saturn starts the gravel
at the end of the driveway crunches as she backs over it.
She drives forty-five minutes to her office complex in a
suburb of Frankenstein City. She spends all day there
perhaps makes one call home or to his office if it's a day

he'll be in his office to say hello. She's home by five or six on a good day. Seven or eight on others. The Wife is a number cruncher. The Wife hates crunching numbers. The Wife hates her company. He's no help with job security money he wouldn't offer a safety net if she were to strike out into something someplace else. He's not exactly a real person if that makes sense. She stays put.

3/07 although Dom's heard a key twisting at first to
lock then getting the idea unlock what was an unlocked
door he still looks up with surprise as he pushes in briefcase first. Dom's not pulled up into the desk but pushed
back from it far enough so his feet are firmly planted
around it one leg in the desk's cubbyhole the other at a
right angle. His right hand holds a black BIC pen his
signature grading implement no other will do he's never
asked why. Exams spread across his desk. Dom doesn't
like exams doesn't like grading them but he's learned from
semesters teaching what he teaches business writing
students will raise hell if he doesn't offer them. Exams.
Class isn't a fair deal unless it involves hard and fast yeses
nos not the vagaries of writing it's not how they put it
Dom's told him but the general idea. He's seen Dom one
other time this week like today their office hours over-
lapped. Carol's desk is wedged under the coveted window
Carol they never see her freshman comp classes first thing
in the morning her office hours right after. Carol's stingy
with her time. Teaching for her is an academic scholarship
an assistantship not a job. She's still in everyone's minds
theirs hers the powers-that-be a student herself. Teaching
for him for Dom shouldn't be a job either but they're older
married Dom with kids teaching more more different
courses different responsibilities it feels like a job. They're

The Chronicle of Higher Education Date: May 30, 1997 Section: Opinion Page: B3 LETTERS TO THE EDITOR The Job Market for Professors To the Editor: 1. The job market is bad, and it has been bad in literature and language since 1970. There are now 35 years of Ph.D.'s who didn't get jobs or who took short-term or adjunct jobs. Several years ago I heard from a former colleague at another college that he was a security guard at a retirement home. His Ph.D. from the University of Wisconsin at Madison was no ticket to academic success in the 1970s. 2. There are 20 Ph.D. students from the English department at the University of California at Los Angeles on the job market. Overproduction by any department is an exploitation of graduate students. 3. We must ask how many of the 1,186 positions listed in the Modern Language Association's "Job Information List" were "empty"—positions for which departments had already made their choices through informal searches or which were ultimately closed because administrators would rather employ cheaper adjunct faculty members. 4. Retirements and turnovers reported in various studies are not being filled at most colleges and universities. Instead, the bare-bones teaching function of those retired professors is being "covered" more and more by part-time adjuncts. 5. In a tight job market, marriages are even more at risk than are individuals. Increasingly, successful academics face the choice of either commuter relationships or the second-class academic citizenship of adjunct teaching positions, a disproportionate percentage of which in the arts and humanities just happen to be filled by women.

dissertating in the final stages of apprenticeship no classes to take so they teach maybe three even four courses a semester. Their committees expect if not an opus a solid book eventually publishable. It's taking several years. In the meantime this office it has a hard feel to it tiled floors cinder block walls painted white they all three share a metal bookcase but no computer. At better moments he thinks it's appropriate. Ascetic. Just right for people who need to concentrate at worse he's embarrassed when students come by what they must think of this the brutest of brute reality. No frills for the undeserving. It makes him feel old. Too old for this sort of thing a failure at thirty-something. He keeps mints in his desk thinking that even his breath smells tired his back often does he wears black shoes the tips scuffed and scratched. The right needs a new lace the end run over by the vacuum cleaner he'll get around to it. There's nothing extraordinary about any of this. Nothing. Maybe his committee maybe his and Dom's committees suspect they're dicking around on stagnant projects biding their final days in the academy in repression useful only as cheap labor. Well maybe not so much with Dom. Hey he says.

11/20 if not the tv then the computer which goes on mornings to stay on all day. A multicolored cube three-dimensional floats across the screen. He runs Windows 95 pirated a gift from his Dissertation Advisor who as The Advisor has gotten from him enough free computer troubleshooting that the OS wasn't a gift but payola. He's not an expert to have been troubleshooting but he knows the basics and he's more often than he should got time on his hands he enjoys fidgeting fussing screwing with hardware software until he gets things right at least working. First things first the computer's power on-off button jerry-rigged at a tilt its mechanisms exposed not quite right since he replaced the power supply. The screen clicks flickers the computer beeps honks hums parts spin. Icon Shortcut to U of F Double click Connect Status Dialing Icon Pegasus Mail for Win32 Double click Wait Toolbar Running C:\Program Files\Accessories\UnixScript Connected at 57600 bps Duration: 000.00.07+ Red Globe Check your Pop3 host for new mail Message bar. Checking host for new mail Identifying unread messages Downloading 1+ of 29 messages his messages filter into appropriate folders and when the numbers to the right of those folders turn green and increase clicking up until all messages are accounted for he knows his lit discussion groups have been busy there's no message from The Advisor

nothing from his brother or parents a stray message from
Gene from freshman writing it's in the New Mail box
unclassifiable. The messages he scans doesn't read because it's morning he's unfocused. Gene wants an extension on his paper. Icon Netscape Communicator Double
Click Wait Bookmarks The New York Times on the Web
Visit briefly Academe Today Visit briefly Link to job
advertisements Browse Alt-X Publishing Network Visit
Browse Not Bookmarked In location box, type: http://
www.voyeurweb.com. He's visited a lot of different sites
on the web in the past how many. Four or five years. Free
software sites bookstore sites gaming sites he's visited
MOOs MUDs MUVs. He's browsed through a pictorial tour
of an abandoned missile silo visited homepages online
family photo albums signed online guest books. He's
gotten medical advice checked the progress of his mutual
fund. He's read the news. He's followed discussions on
Homicide NYPD Blue Saved by the Bell of all things he's
obsessed with Screech. Who isn't. He's seen spread legs
spread lips gaping anuses with fists in them blowjobs
bondage simulated rapes fucking sucking foot fetishes
piercings waifs animals orgies tag-team intercourse in live-
time feed complete with sound bleached-blondes with red
painted lips semen stretching from their squinting eyes to
their mouths. He knows where the porno sites are who
doesn't he's visited them all. He doesn't hang around them
not because he's a prude not because he's afraid of getting
caught by The Wife the U of F computer accountmaster if
there is such a thing. These sites aren't interesting. Human
livestock shows. Professionals leering and pouting and
licking and pumping and sucking and groping and stroking and squatting and squeezing and screwing. Their faces
above their tanned bodies are empty male and female
alike. But The Voyeurweb. Photos at The Voyeurweb are
private taken of lovers and spouses present and former
and strangers some with a subject's permission. Others
without. Mostly without. There are lingerie shots shots of

women in showers coming out of showers shots of
women dressing undressing sunbathing shots upskirt shots
downblouse shots of lighted windows without curtains.
There are shots of women sleeping and shots of nude
beaches. There are hidden camera shots of couples
fucking. It's embarrassing he thinks his fascination with
The Voyeurweb it suggests something unhealthy about
him. He decides again and again he won't visit the site.
He always returns. He likes to watch. He wants what he
watches to be real and there's reality at The Voyeurweb
that can't be found in tv and even perhaps in real life. In a
way if that makes sense it makes sense to him. The real in
real life isn't real almost never does he does anyone get to
see behind behind the scenes. When we do he thinks we
usually know so well or think we do what we see that it's
got no interest it's not really behind the scenes. At least
this is how he understands things he loves The
Voyeurweb's images of stolen frozen moments of
unselfconsciousness thoughtlessness of just being unaware
of being watched even by oneself watching oneself being
watched by others. Being in every sense being incautious.
He understands also that he might be a very small man
but understanding doesn't always equal knowing. He
collects on his hard drive copies of his favorite Voyeurweb
pictures. According to its counters The Voyeurweb re-
ceives two hundred thousand visitors a day.

No date it will take him a second after he clicks in to realize what's odd about the party. What it is is there'll be about a half dozen people there and only one will be a girl. The brunette in pigtails and shorts and white blouse they'll meet at the door will be the same Midwestern farm girl dancing excitedly with two men in the center of the room. The girl with flushed cheeks who will ask them if they're all friends will be the girl staring at them from the other side of the room with eyes that are too deep. And will be the same girl kissing an older Mr. Magoo of a man in the corner and then a little later squirming on the lap of the bland man with light brown hair khaki pants an oxford button-down not buttoned all the way up. The fat man in blue shirt and hat is meant to look jolly but he's not when you really look creases corner his mouth. The fat man's little buddy is meant to look scared but he's not he seems hard and mean with his little sailor's cap. The walls are thatch it's a hut but if he could see through the door when it opens he sees a bare room well lighted it's a studio floodlamps expensive digital cameras mounted on tripods. This is not The Voyeurweb. This is a professional production. He's not sure why he's here he's not sure he has what it takes to stay. Processor speed is the least of his worries. The girl looks like one of his students she's incredibly cute every class meeting it's what he thinks she's fantastically cute.

The little buddy. Gee, you sure are cute.

Girl. Looks coyly at her feet. So are you.

The little buddy. You know how much we all like you.

Girl. I guess.

The bland man. Better than the other two, to be sure.

Mr. Magoo. I should say. Much better.

Girl. Flashes sunny smile. I like you all too.

The jolly fat man. Well why don't you show us.

The camera connected at high speed to the internet follows them as they form a circle sitting on crude stools the girl sits more or less in the center cheeks red eyes glittering and her deep nipples show brown now through her blouse. A hand covers her breast it's the bland man she closes her eyes opens them doesn't move.

Mr. Magoo. We should have done this a long time ago.

Girl. We haven't done anything yet.

The bland man lifts her other breast she takes a deep breath doesn't exhale. Mr. Magoo pulls her over and gives her a long kiss she's pulled back flat by several hands.

Girl. Oh, finally, thank god.

Oh finally thank god hands pull at her clothing at a sign from the jolly fat man. Still wearing her underpants she takes a directed pose in the middle of the circle of hands the actors pretend to admire her long repressed lust finally given over. He stares for once without embarrassment shyness shame. Hands close in to pull her down. The bland man feeds her his cock. Mr. Magoo bends to lick between her legs. The jolly fat man twists her around a careful maneuver to give him access to her ass penetrates her rear. Eventually the little buddy pretends to get over some fear there's a pause the focus is on him. He takes off his shirt skin and bones. He unzips. He's going to Give It To Her. The main attraction hung like a horse. He's a star.

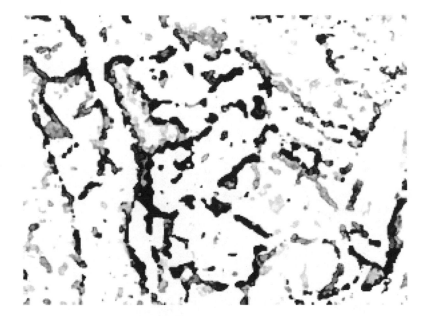

4/09 around five he clicks off the tv stands up. A
sliver of the floor is yellow with afternoon sun. On goes
the stereo the CD player a disc pulled out and clicked into
the nearest case. Another disc in the player and music in
the living room. The wire stretched half the length of the
apartment running along the baseboards and near the
ceiling means music from the kitchen speakers too.

Fellows I'm ready to get up and do my thing.

Oh yeah do your thing.

Two glasses smudged with grease on the coffee
table not really a coffee table but the seat of a discarded
futon frame it has legs he hammered on and a chipped
sheet of glass on top. One mug a tea bag in it on the end
table.

I want to get into it, man, you know,

go ahead

On the coffee table and the floor next to it two days of
newspapers and catalogs from L.L.Bean Victorian Paper
Company PBS Home Video Nancy's Notions MacWarehouse
MicroWarehouse J.Crew Sierra Trading Post Daedalus
Books. Magazines. The New Yorker. Self. Shape. Harper's.
The newspaper goes in the recycling bin. Everything else
will be piled straightened then left alone.

like a, like a sex machine, man,

oh yeah go ahead

His shoes next to the chair. The Wife's cross-trainers by the sofa.

movin', doin' it, you know.

Yeah

Forget the dining room the library books and computer disks and student papers they'll eat in the living room tonight again. Watch the news and

Can I count it off.

Go ahead

in the kitchen he'll wash the dishes and wipe the counters and maybe he should run to the store before The Wife gets home to get some bread to have with the fettuccine and garlic and olive oil and Parmesan. Maybe in a bag a salad too.

One

She'll be home at six tonight.

Two

That gives him some time. Maybe he'll check his email.

Three

The Wife was grumpy when she called the stupid fucks in her office.

Four

He can read tonight prepare class while The Wife watches tv. Maybe a little tv after she goes to bed. Maybe instead he'll tape Letterman and watch it tomorrow.

mBupBupBup

What The Wife does for her salary.

BupBupBup

Maybe he'll check The Voyeurweb.

BupBupBaaahhhh

She'll take it out on him tonight what she puts up with. For her salary. There's no logic in her anger at him. He could make a good living she'd still work she wants to work and it means crunching numbers and putting up with shitheads commuting long distances. But she'll be angry anyway because there's no logic to unhappiness she thinks she's doing her best why aren't things better it must be his fault somehow they could have more be more what exactly. He doesn't know he imagines himself entering their home evenings smiling briefcase in hand stumbling over the ottoman The Wife watches lovingly says Oh You Silly.

He's got a few minutes. Maybe he'll beat off. Get up.

07/07 *OPENING CREDITS OVER*: (INT. LOBBY OF
HIS AND THE WIFE'S APARTMENT BUILDING). Ned
rings. When the security door buzzes Ned comes in but
not up. His head tilted Ned looks up the stairs shouts Liz
is double-parked out front.

HIM: We'll be right down.

The Wife is ready behind him inside their door. She
steps out purse on arm pulls out her keys.

Hang on he says working backwards. I'll just be a
second.

The Wife calls down. Hi Ned.

He walks quickly to the back bedroom. The lights are
off. He turns them on and then off. In the bathroom he
pees it's an effort. He's too young to have prostate disease
it must be nerves. From the front hall The Wife asks what
he's doing it's what he thinks she says. He can't hear her
clearly. He rinses his hands wipes them turns off the light.
In the kitchen the coffeemaker is definitely off. The gas on
the stove is definitely off. He checks the locks on the back
door.

THE WIFE: Come on. They're waiting.

Ok he says I'm right behind you.

While the wife starts down he checks his computer.
It's unplugged. In case of thunderstorms what else has he
forgotten to take care of he does a double take body

jerking back slaps the heel of his hand to his forehead laughter from the audience walks back through the apartment closing windows. He has no idea what's forecasted for the evening. It's hot in any case it'll be hot when they return humid the apartment like the inside of a mouth. He considers leaving on the air conditioner in the bedroom. Maybe not. What if. What if what he doesn't know maybe a short circuit a fire maybe a condensation leak the bedroom flooded he doesn't turn it on. One light on in the living room. No need for a coat. He opens the closet door anyway and stares this is all very funny it's meant to be. This fussiness is also a little sad if seen right he stares for a second too long maybe he wants to crawl in there himself the shot lingers as he steps back sighs closes the door. Shrugs his shoulders ho hum and now it's just funny again. Cut to: He steps into the landing jangling his keys The Wife and Ned are talking in the foyer. They stop and look up at him.

Sorry he says. He locks the top bolt once unlock and once again then the lower switch cranking until it catches pulling the door tight into its frame. Be right there. He imagines fears The Wife and Ned are rolling their eyes. This is not a fear based in reality. They wouldn't do that. But it's exactly what they are doing mugging their movements exaggerated The Wife taps the toes of her shoe crosses her arms rolls her eyes again makes a face it's all very comical. Ned gives her a resigned smile tilting his head what can you do it says his body language. Downstairs (EXT. FRONT OF BUILDING AND STREET) he sees that they're already getting in the car. Ned's given The Wife the front seat so he arranges himself with Ned in the rear knees pressed in. He's not uncomfortable it's not far to the restaurant or later to the movies. If they're up for it. But he wriggles for effect can't seem to get comfortable his knees dig into the seat in front of him The Wife wants to know what he's Doing Back There. He resigns himself with a snort Elizabeth looks back at Ned puts the car into gear laughter from offstage.

LIZ: How are you it's been so long since we've gotten together I feel like it's been a year.

THE WIFE: Yes. My God. Last time was what how long.

LIZ: Like months. How are you what have you been up to. It's been so crazy. Ned and I feel like we never have a spare minute.

Ned grins nods to him tiny laugh. Time just disappears.

Affable he shakes his head. He agrees. Not really time for him often lingers but he doesn't have a line to this effect there's no time now to comment on the script. This isn't a dress rehearsal this is the real thing. Showtime. And he's supposed to agree so he agrees. They're all in agreement.

When did he and The Wife lose their personal friends the *personal* friends belonging to one or the other of them but not both. Friends moved away or they did. Friends became a part of couples available only as a team effort their names linked in double-dactyls. ErikandEmily RobertandStephanie NedandElizabeth.

At dinner (INT. RESTAURANT—STREETLAMPS IN DARK OUTSIDE WINDOW. EXTRAS AT ADJOINING TABLES) he sits across from Ned who sits next to Liz who sits across from The Wife who sits next to him. The Trattoria isn't expensive but not cheap. It's big with open rooms. On the walls hang famous prints tastefully framed. A huge papier-mâché eggplant sits in one corner a tomato in another. An enormous green pepper by the bar the audience is hushed waiting for them to speak. They don't at first there's a pause as they settle in in their first seminar together he and Ned studied Lacan and contemporary British lit. The Wife had been The Fiancé and Ned had had no partner this in montage images flashbacks popping into view one into the next into the next. During and then after the seminar he and Ned's friends Garag and Michelle Goethe Stephanie St. Michael and sometimes The Fiancé drank beer in Ned's apartment on weekends watched tv cooked out on his tiny back porch. They tried to keep their feet from Ned's dog kicked as a pup before he'd been found by Ned he started life as a toe biter. Feet moved he bit feet didn't move he watched for moving feet. Ned took up fishing their second year he went along sometimes not to catch fish but to bullshit about graduate school and women and the advantages of pissing out-doors. Once they went hiking in Frankenstein's largest forest preserve not finding a water supply three then four hours into the woods. When Ned met Elizabeth she was a graduate student in architecture. Now she works like the Wife this isn't necessary too somber. Shouldn't be drawn out short cut he didn't like Titanic but Elizabeth did with qualifications of course it was a spectacle after all The Wife agrees mostly. Ned shrugs grins says he thinks Leo is just marv. Big laughs. Elizabeth says Oh You pokes him The Wife wants to know how was their trip they visited Elizabeth's family. Everyone agrees before saying no more that working nine to five isn't the finest thing in the world. Laughs Oh You Know It Girl.

Ned is flying to the East Coast to deliver a paper not a big deal he says and The Wife says that's great. It's clear that Ned is going to be as successful as he's always wanted to be then no one says anything. He coughs drops his napkin bends to pick it up wonders about Ned and Elizabeth's sex life. They're not kinky types not photo-takers. But he'd like to see Elizabeth on the Voyeurweb in fact thinks he has seen her ass toward the camera a smidgen of blondish hair poking out between her white white ass cheeks her tits hanging down as she bends to pick up a sock he's lounging in bed. All afternoon they've been fucking his cock is chafed and red. He's taking surreptitious photos with a digital camera hipshots. The camera makes no shutter sounds he must have a dozen photos. He's got her number he shifts uncomfortably in his seat. A shock runs through the audience they're aware of the bulge in his pants no. They're not they can't be he moves his napkin on his lap. Oh oh. There's a big stain on his pants a half a meatball has fallen from his fork and he's trying to hide the mess how embarrassing. Laughter big big big laughs. Elizabeth and The Wife puzzle over the check. Ned raises his eyebrows and smiles wondering why's he so quiet tonight. Who knows he does he's not saying. After a vote they decide they'll see the new Harrison Ford flick a no-brainer but good for Saturday night something effortless after a week of hard work. He orders a huge popcorn no butter shares it with everyone. He drinks a huge diet Coke has to pee at a crucial moment a little comic relief. Ha ha. When Ned and Elizabeth drop them off their car blocks the small street its blinkers flashing and everyone says good-bye. Upstairs The Wife doesn't notice the VCR it's taping Saturday Night Live. It's time for bed. (FADE OUT. END OF SHOW.)

5/15 he and The Wife have sex once a week Satur-
days late morning or afternoon. They've never had much
sex it's not him maybe The Wife doesn't like it had a bad
experience. She's never told him. Maybe they understand
it differently. He's not sure he understands it at all and
doesn't want to wants to just do it and that's the appeal.
Maybe she thinks she understands it too well. What is it
she understands. Their story started with nervousness
where she was still and he moved a lot segued to nervousness she was less still but still still and he didn't move
as much and then they had fun for a while. But it didn't
last. Sometimes he's on top. She's on top when she's got
the energy to bring herself to orgasm. The Wife doesn't
like oral sex. They're friendly enough during talking as
they take care of business. It doesn't take long. End of
story. Is it.

10/26 in Finch's copy of *98.6* the "Frankenstein"
section is marked with black pen. "Children of Frankenstein" is marked in blue. "Palestine" in red. Words phrases
sentences are underlined a shorthand version of the novel.
On page three Finch wanted to remember that You intuit.
That's how you do it. On page four that The Ancien Caja
is What he's looking for. On page three that the Ancien
Caja is Of the earth. That the earth teaches us that Death is
power and that Only those who know it can survive and
then only for a while no escape. On page eight that in the
face of Death he's Waiting for the unexpected the aberra-
tion the extraordinary event the one chance in a million
that will allow him if he's alert enough to slip through.
Putting his faith in the unknown. On pages nine and ten a
line curves around the text that says Frankenstein is racing
like a wheel out of contact with the ground a loose
flywheel spinning faster and faster till it tears the whole
machine apart. Now he knows he's back in his life and
after all he learned everything is the same as before. Only
worse. On page eleven He thinks that the extraordinary
is the answer to The Problem. He believes in powers
meaning the extension of the ordinary to the point of the
incredible and he believes that these powers are real
though they can't be willed and they belong to everyone
who isn't blinded by negative hallucinations of our

swears
deep
as a
all the
with
own.
heel
either
den.
he's

10/23 he has a thing and that is that he's only interested in
the extraordinary. He thinks that the extraordinary is the
answer to The Problem. For example he'd rather sit home
and watch the hummingbird at the feeder outside his window
than go through the motions of a common seduction with
nothing special about it. Hummingbirds are special birds the
way dolphins are special animals they have a certain perspective a kind of openendedness about their intelligence that
makes him feel kin. Ariel was a hummingbird. He believes
in powers meaning the extension of the ordinary to the point
of the incredible and he believes that these powers are real
though they can't be willed and they belong to everyone who
isn't blinded by the negative hallucination of our culture. A
negative hallucination is when you don't see something that's
really there. He still has negative hallucinations but is trying
to get rid of them. Like when The Witch suddenly says what
he's thinking he never bothers to ask how did you know. Or
when something is lost and he inexplicably knows where it is
he no longer finds it disturbing. Or when he walks into a store
in New York to buy a pair of shoes and he meets a friend he
hasn't seen in five years and who is in Paris and only passing
through the city for two hours neither are surprised because
this kind of thing happens to both of them all the time. He
believes that to get rid of negative hallucination you have to
be enchanted. He believes that all people need to enchant
their lives but that only those succeed who neither search nor
close their minds but simply remain open to the unknown.
He thinks that this is the source of all civilization. People also
have the power to enchant one another and when this hap-

culture. A negative hallucination is when you don't see
something that's really there. He still has negative hallucinations but is trying to get rid of them. Pen brackets the
moments when he has gotten rid of them. On page twelve
a curve boldly checked. It emphasizes that When people
are not in touch it's dull and sometimes painful that when
this occurs on a mass scale as he thinks it has the only
resort is to The Ancien Caja the extraordinary it's not sex
that's extraordinary it's the extraordinary that's extraordinary. The point is that sex is the only thing we can't do
without that has to be either extraordinary or hellish so it
brings up all the problems this is what the book says. Is
this true. That in the long run there's only love and hate.
Well if you can't go around it go through it. That's how
you do it. Love conks us all. The hello embrace Ned gives
The Witch lasts an instant too long and the intimacy of his
handshake and smile as if they share something makes
him wonder whether he ever slept with her. They are
entering a phase in their affair when power relations are
shifting he is no longer god the father not that he ever
wanted to be it's just that she resents that he ever was. He
understands wondering about Ned she might no longer
always tell him the truth or rather she might consider that
the truth is not always his business. Finch didn't mark the
transcript describing this guy's cold sperm it's just one of
many things he didn't mark this irritates him it in fact bugs
him beyond measure. Why. Jealousy he's lost the ability to
pick and choose with Sukenick he can't select some things
Sukenick's written and ignore others. His first copy of *98.6*
the one he turns to again and again when thinking about
writing about Sukenick has gotten harder and harder to
read now it's almost impossible every line is underlined
his own handwriting crowds the margins. Highlighters
were for a while helpful they ended up turning the book
into a rainbow of colors competing for attention. He
doesn't remember what the different colors were meant to
signify in the first place if yellow lines are more important

than blue are these more important than orange. How do you write a dissertation in the face of this he's lost in the text. You have a few beers he thinks you pick a Sukenick text and copy it word for word verbatim transcription. You turn it in as your dissertation. The idea makes him laugh why not go one step further copy *98.6* word for word providing critical detachment in the footnotes what a gas. Why stop there is what he thinks why not fit the footnotes into the text itself make them part of it plagiarizing Sukenick here and offering himself there now it's fiction now criticism some theoretical speculations maybe a little of this a little of that. Fat chance. Not the kind of thing to pass through his committee. You don't get a Ph.D. on a lark.

6/5 Sukenick notes Palenque Aztec equals death.
Maya equals death.

Aztec equals the weight of the pyramid on the tiny chamber in its base where you wait.

Maya equals the dream that you can escape that there is an unknown passageway that the pyramid is a dream from which you can awake.

Maya equals the man and woman standing naked in front of their thatched hut at midday in the jungle.

Aztec equals the men with no expression on their faces who close around you in the jungle night.

Aztec equals all in one Coatlicue the beheaded with two heads the twin rattlesnakes of schizophrenia with claws of death with necklace of hearts with belt of skull with skirt of snakes spider hands instead of breasts her talons imprison the earth the war god is her son we are all her children.

Maya equals the parts the many the Chac and Yum Kaax also Ix Tab and Ah Puch also Ix Chel and Shoosh Ek and the four Chaques and Ik and the four Iques and the nine inferior heavens also the sacred tree of life its roots in the world of death and its branches reaching toward the thirteen superior heavens.

Maya equals children selling flowers.

Aztec equals men with eyes like the wrong end of a telescope.

Aztec equals monolith.
Maya equals rise and fall rise and fall rise and fall.
Maya equals escape by water.
Aztec equals flat.
Maya equals fluid Italian the underworld.
Aztec equals German stiff the police.
Aztec equals mastery.
Maya equals mystery.
Aztec equals the stone knife that distinguishes the heart from the body it samples the blood till knowledge is complete that's the way it makes love.

Maya equals the living virgins pushed into the water of the sacred Cenote to make love with the rain god "who don't die though they never see them again."[1]

Aztec equals death.
Maya equals death.

---

[1] Bishop Landa being quoted in *98.6* being quoted in *Guía Oficial de Chichen Itza*, 9th edition, Instituo Nacional de Antropología e Historia (Mexico, D.F., March 1969), p. 11. (Translation and punctuation his.)

"The Problem," as he puts it, is that Frankenstein is a world in which information is supplied by the news media, "ABC network news feature pyramids," and the information supplied is likely to be about new directions in an insatiable consumer desire for goods (and who can tell whether the news media report or create this desire); the pyramids discussed by ABC News "are the latest consumer craze sweeping the nation an actress rests her chin on a small pyramid while sleeping to prevent wrinkles fruit is said to ripen more quickly inside pyramidal structures" (6). Frankenstein is, according to Sukenick, a world in which "people are not in touch it's dull and sometimes painful" and happening on a mass scale (11). Or, rather, Frankensteinians have a mass of scales before their eyes and are subject to *negative hallucinations*, which happen "when you don't see something *that's really there*" (11) [italics mine]. What is really there, according to "him," is possibility, coincidence, even magic—the extraordinary. This possibility is ground out of Frankensteinians, who like the average Americans of Sukenick's <u>Out</u>, tour the country in their rumpus-room equipped recreational vehicles arguing about whether their kids are glandular or fat—and this when the typical father is not slamming these kids "in the stomach with his fist" (<u>OUT</u> 153).

That "pyramids" are the latest consumer craze is, of course, significant because for "him," pyramids symbolize "The Answer" to "The Problem." This answer, for the narrator, is "The Ancien Caja," a becoming-earthly; this Ancien Caja is "of the earth…heavy scaled with rust and mold buried" (5). It is primitivism, nature, the reality of death, the extraordinary. The Ancien Caja is, in fact, like many things (just as are The Problem and The Answer); it is "like the jungle air filled with butterflies…like the slow throbbing of the fountain of blood in your hard prick your cranky mind for once asleep in the cradle of your body. It's like the narrow hewn steps under massive stone blocks…like the secret code on the leopard's fur and the tortoise shell" (4).

The Ancien Caja is not actually even "like" these many things, but it "is" these many things. In <u>98.6</u>, the Ancien Caja operates as an abstract machine, and it is not "a designation of something by means of a proper name, nor an assignation of metaphor by means of a figurative sense," but instead an abstraction of "a sequence of intensive states…no longer in the situation of an ordinary, rich language where the word dog, for example, would directly designate an animal and would apply metaphorically to other things (so one could say 'like a dog')" (<u>Kafka</u> 21-22). When "he" refers to the Ancien Caja, there is "no longer a subject of the enunciation, nor a subject of the statement. Rather, there is a circuit of states that forms a mutual becoming, in the heart of a necessarily multiple or collective assemblage" (<u>Kafka</u> 22).

"Even he doesn't know what The Ancien Caja is. Exactly" (12). This is because in <u>98.6</u>, The Ancien Caja is not a thing or even a reference to a thing, but rather a metamorphic metaphor, and it describes the ways in which a series of terms, ideas, and ideals shift and change in meaning as the relationships between "things" change. Sukenick, like Wallace Stevens, does not operate dialectically, bringing opposites into agreement, but rather "his syntheses are momentary, unstable, and, instead of advancing his argument, always break down…. That is why the relation between such terms must constantly be restated" (In Form 163). The Ancien Caja *is* the imagination grappling with something *other* than that which is normally understood—a sense of possibility and the extraordinary. And, as a sense which "he" pursues, it is continually redefined as he approaches and/or swerves away from it—made concrete only by his imaginative renderings of what he perceives to be his experiential contacts with it.

In its footnotes (which, appearing in a "novel," help Sukenick to disorient commonsensical notions of what properly belongs in a fictional text and a nonfiction or autobiographical work), 98.6 indicates that the notion of the Ancien Caja springs from the narrator's (and by extension Sukenick's) research into the Aztec and Mayan civilizations, which had in their times faced, respectively, the type of crushing stagnancy in which Frankenstein is currently mired as well as the possibilities of a different, and "enchanted" civilization.[2] It's in the Aztec civilization that "he" sees an entire spectrum of situations engendered both by "A civilization so deadened by its own proliferation that only death can renew its commitment to life," and in the Mayan civilization a state of existence whose inhabitants have access to the Ancien Caja, the extraordinary, and who "simply remain open to the unknown" (7, 11).[3] In other words, "he" sees the lure of the Ancien Caja as being extraordinarily intense for inhabitants of a Frankensteinian State that channels desire into a desire for commercial goods, a need for freeway speed, and is predicated upon silent and cruel violence, built by "men with eyes like the

---

[2] In addition to blurring generic distinctions, the use of footnotes in 98.6 also suggests the very coincidental origins of the novel—that its entire inspiration was sparked by Sukenick's chance interest the footnoted books The Development of Early Pre-Columbian Architecture and Sexual Behavior in the Human Female. That is, if certain focal ideas from which 98.6 sprang came from the books in the footnotes, then Sukenick is complicating the relationship between supposedly primary and supposedly secondary texts: Which, 98.6 seems to ask, do you think is which? Even though footnoted, are the texts in question more important somehow than the main text itself? Or perhaps should such distinctions be rendered moot?

[3] The first quote is taken from Foster Linkletter's The Development of Early Pre-Columbian Architecture (New York: New York University Press, 1948), 27. Punctuation is "his."

9/16 the couch is expensive it's older than their
married life. Day one in their new apartment a half-year
from the wedding The Wife fixed on it as an idea and
announced that they would get a nice one. Weekdays and
even weekends or parts of them taken over by her new
job they searched out furniture stores when they could.
Evenings when The Wife wasn't too tired she leafed
through catalogs. The sofa is cream colored with wide
blue and green striping and fat arms. It's from IKEA. He's
never thought it very soft but it is nice handsome the best
piece of furniture they own. The Wife is home fifty waking hours a week. She likes the sofa it's against the wall
halfway down from the living room windows across from
the tv. The tv is mid-range Sony a bargain he hunted
down at an electronics superstore. Ditto the vcr. The
stereo's old a college purchase. They have a nice mattress
set. Sealy. Eight hundred dollars. Their dining room table
is square hardwood a present from his parents. St. Mike
doesn't say anything when he comes over for coffee but
looking around the apartment not looking he seems to
think the walls are too bare the rooms too empty. Seems
to wonder why there are so few plants not a knickknack
in sight. St. Mike's too poor to buy nice things and what
he can afford he doesn't acquire because he's not settled.
But a certain amount of creative accumulation can't hurt.

Throw dispensable things out or rummage them off when you move. The kitchen pantry the fridge are full of food. He's twenty pounds overweight. The Wife thirty. He and St. Mike drink Guatemalan Oriflama. St. Mike describes the paranoid impulses in three films he's studying tells him about finding a movie version of a novel by Sukenick. If he's interested. He brews a second pot when they mostly St. Mike finish the first. Six feet something and big but not fat St. Mike drinks coffee with breakfast at mid-morning at lunch through the afternoon after supper and in the evening while he writes. Still he speaks slowly. His hands don't shake. His mind is alert always. He doesn't sleep more than six hours a night is what he says. Maybe St. Mike will die at an early age. St. Mike is a half chapter and a full revision away from defending his dissertation. He's twenty-seven. St. Mike knows what he's doing around him always there's a sense of confident forward motion. He'll have his hood by Christmas a job in fall. He looks up to St. Mike wants to be like him. He can't be like him if he believes what Sukenick says that the point is to avoid the point to be always in the middle in flight. That it's not enough to say down with genres one must effectively write in such a way there are no more genres etc. It's a lot of bs insanity he knows you can't get anywhere thinking like this you can't finish a dissertation. But that's the point to go nowhere and end up somewhere else. What the fuck does that mean he wishes he were somewhere else he's just not very good at getting there. Where. And why not. He's not sure. This morning is the third in a row that in the glue traps he found mouse shit but no mice.

3/23 what everyone knows is this If Basil Utter is on your committee and your dissertation satisfies his demands you're doing well you will do well. This everyone knows because everyone knows this too Basil Utter is brilliant and famous and rigorous to a fault. Many suspect this also You don't fuck around around Basil Utter. Basil is not interested in what doesn't feel right right to him personally even if what's right is wrong. He knows the difference. Basil's not patient with what he suspects he's heard before even if he has said said thing. Basil is married to a gorgeous woman twenty years his junior Kristine Olmos-Utter also brilliant a full professor if not distinguished. Basil is secretly annoyed when dissertations are written about those he considers his inferiors. Basil Utter will be seventy-six in the fall. Basil intimidates The Advisor and The Advisor hates being cowed. The Advisor frowns at Basil's ego. The Advisor avoids Basil's company. He considers on rare occasions that in ten years he'll be healthy and attending Basil's funeral commemorating a great man artist scholar. This last he reminds himself of when smiling grimly no ill will involved but an ironic detachment from the grim reality of the earth and a humility his demeanor recognizing the inevitability of betrayal the sadness of all things. His youngest children from his second marriage are the same age as Basil's youngest child from his second marriage. His temperature is 98.6. In Basil's office on a late afternoon of spring Basil sits across from him a groomed terrier curled up by the door. What Basil tells him about his dissertation evenly pausing now and then for any feedback that might be right enough and new enough for him to mention if he so desires is that

He doesn't see a compelling reason for so much Deleuze and Guattari

Sukenick's dissociative model of narration is in many ways similar to the discursive mode employed by poststructuralist collaborators Deleuze and Guattari. Consistently pushing, in thought and practice, toward "extricating [themselves] from the problems of anti-Hegelianism and constructing an alternative train of thought," Deleuze and Guattari's work attempts to construct a "non-dialectical conception of negation and a constitutive theory of practice" which takes immanence and immanent interpretation as a crucial tenet.

This post-Hegelian philosophy theorizes that positive, liberated creation is possible when "pure" negation, or extreme nihilism, clears a space for new being. As Michael Hardt says in his study of Gilles Deleuze, Deleuze's philosophy does not advocate pure negation, pure nihilism, but recognizes it as an inevitable "element of our world". This absolute Deleuzian negation, with its continual movement toward ground-zero, so to speak, does not work toward nihilism as an end, however. Instead, it is pursued so that alternative geographical terrains for thought and action can be opened and reopened.

The perpetual "clearing" of such spaces, for Deleuze and Guattari, is intrinsically related to a desire-driven constructivism. This constructivism can take advantage of these leveled spaces, exploring and creating anew, and it frequently grapples with, as Sukenick's fictions consistently and dynamically do, basic questions of ontology: what is the nature of being, in what world does this being take place, and what world suits particular moments. The impossibility of finding foundational answers to these questions, in the face of an always-present potential of profound negation, leads to perpetual immanence, a perpetual rethinking and re-creating in each succeeding moment "the relationship between language, literature, thought, desire, action, social institutions, and material reality" (Bogue 7-8).

DeleuzeGuattarian poststructuralism and contemporary surfiction typically:

> ...limit us to a strictly immanent and
> materialist ontological discourse that refuses
> any deep or hidden foundation of being. There
> is nothing veiled or negative about [immanent]
> being; it is fully expressed in the world.
> Being, in this sense, is superficial, positive,
> and full.... The radical negation of the
> nondialectical *pars destruens* emphasizes that
> no preconstituted order is available to define
> the organization of being. Practice provides
> the terms of a material *pars construens*;
> practice is what makes the constitution of
> being possible. (Hardt xiii)

The impulse arising from immanence, claim Deleuze and Guattari, is a will to power—a will to power not *over* others or the world, but a will to create new values. This will to power celebrates difference, both in the self and in cultural regimes, by enacting difference, and by attempting to exist outside of "preexisting social orders" (McGowan 81). Immanent constructions, or interpretations, are attentive to possibility rather than any previously assumed "reality," and they reflect an aesthetic of "libidinal politics," or a politics of desire. Associated with Kristeva and Foucault as well as Deleuze and Guattari this politics of desire describes the liberation of immanence finding its actuality in transgressive action, which takes many forms and is a release of the body's desiring intensities, intensities which these thinkers believe to have been restricted and deformed by modernity's creation, control, and repression of the subject. These are "modes of immediate experience as an impulse towards plenitude" (Waugh Practicing 10-11).

Some poststructural conceptions of desire, specifically the DeleuzeGuattarian conception of desire, are complicated by their turn away from the rational subject in which desire has traditionally been located. Distinct from various psychoanalytic understandings of desire—typified by the Freudian definition of desire as a subject's *drive* or in the Lacanian definition of desire as that which arises from some *lack* in the subject which can be

46

He's
beco
ming
more
and
more
conv
ince
d
that
meta
fict
ion
real
ly
is
dead
,
and
so
not
wort
h
anot
her
diss
erta
tion
.
Even
if
meta
fict
ion
were
stil
l
wort
h
anot
her
look

never satisfied, some demand which can never be unambiguously defined and/or fulfilled—Deleuze and Guattari envision desire as "the production of singular states of intensity by the repulsion-attraction of limitative bodies-without-organs (governed by deterministic whole attractors) and non-limitative bodies without organs (governed by chance-ridden fractal attractors)" (Massumi 82). Which is to say, Deleuze and Guattari have reconceptualized desire as a process of production, attraction, repulsion, movement, and composition; desire is a process of multiple, cocausal interactions and becomings not located within or located upon a subject, but made up of freely-moving flows of energy between fragments. Drawing heavily on the Nietzschean perceptions that the world is a "chaos of sensations" where all is always flux, that "no things remain but only dynamic quanta, in a relation of tension to other dynamic quanta," Deleuze and Guattari propose that "nature, then, is an interrelated multiplicity of forces, and all forces are either dominant or dominated. A body is defined by 'this relationship between dominant and dominated forces. Every relationship of force constitutes a body—whether it is chemical, biological, social, or political'" (Will to Power 332-33, 339). In other words, Deleuze and Guattari view desire as flowing from an unconscious that is made up of "primordial states of affective existence…[and] bodily intensities, or punctuated bursts of desiring energies" (Best 83). They understand desire to be

> decentered, fragmented, and dynamic in nature.
> Desire operates in the domain of free synthesis
> where everything is possible and it always
> seeks more objects, connections and relations
> than any socius can allow, pursuing "nomadic and
> polyvocal" rather than segregative and biunivocal
> flows…. [It] is fundamentally positive and
> productive in nature, operating not in search
> of a lost object which would consummate and
> complete it, but out of the productive plenitude
> of its own energy which propels it to seek ever
> new connections and instantiations. (Best 86)

Desire is energy, impulse, creation, and it is acutely important to the body in a plane of immanence, as it is the motivational force which compels that body towards a positive production. Also, desire takes its profitable form in action, in composition rather than contemplation, creation and exploration of difference rather than the organization of difference.

Certain questions will, of course, arise when studying Sukenick. The fact that he strives to reach a plane of immanence does not, of course, mean that he succeeds, and it seems impossible to ignore the arguments of critics like Graff or Wilde, whose sense is that the actual possibilities of reaching an immediacy or immanence which transgresses a Cartesian split between subject and object, mind and body are slim, and that what results from the attempt is merely an anxiety-ridden stream of consciousness.

To these readers, Sukenick is too ratiocinative; his fictions seem to lack a certain affect, and, too smart for their own good, their main emphasis is almost always on being able to exploit a keen understanding of relativism, dodging, as they do, perversely and "confusingly in and out of the logical light, darting into conclusive clarity at one point only to scurry into shadowy contradiction at the next...[so, being] generally counter-intuitive, they [can] always rub against the grain of everyday understanding" (Jackson 30-1). The greatest affective response this likely generates in readers is frustration, if readers bear with the books at all. To paraphrase the sentiment of this argument: if there is affect in the audience it can't just be the frustration of someone whose logic has been tampered with; how often can you tamper with someone's logic, without creating a one-trick pony, and how many people make the kind of sense in the first place that it's so crucial to get readers to *stop making sense* and participate in the foolishness. More commonly, the novels of Sukenick have been understood in the canon of postmodern fiction (in which every new day a fixedness sets in more assuredly) as merely avant-garde experimentations in linguistic improvisation and theory-driven games in genre hybridization and typographical wordplay. They should be seen, however, as functions in schizophrenic flux and fragmentation, their behaviors deliberately and consistently disrupting the literary tradition and the rules of conduct and the language of rationality in order to recurrently enter into an uninterpretable space of desire (the space of the imaginary, for example, or an area of pre-representation), and they should be characterized as such. They are not merely manipulations of already existing forms; they actually strive to *destroy* ordinary language in order to communicate new perceptions of reality, and these perceptions do not base themselves on binaries or

48

dualities, but **are** instead "multiplicities" of immediate experience. The writings of Sukenick exist rhizomatically, thwarting unity and totality by creating *from the middle*, or as Deleuze and Guattari strive to create, from plateaus without beginning or end. In these plateaus, they trace sets of "lines of dimensions which are irreducible to one another"—nets or labyrinths which resemble more the rhizomatic tuber (growing in between other life forms, and from series of buds along its stem) than the tree, which works from root to tip, linearly, and in definable segments (Dialogues vii).

,
perh
aps
Suke
nick
is
not.

These surfictions move incessantly toward a plane of immanence, where traditional notions of organization and development are not conceived, and (written) works (in this case) are assemblages of consistency or composition. They achieve a libidinal frenzy, in fact, on this plane of immanence, "when circumstances combine to bring an activity to a pitch of intensity that is not automatically dissipated in a climax leading to a state of rest" (Massumi 7). This pitch of intensity (plane of immanence, plane of consistency, or plateau), which might be called a style, is an open form, existing continually in a poised or virtual state, receptive to any potentialities. It is a state of indeterminacy both indecisive and ambivalent and receptive to any conceptual possibilities. The texts on a plane of immanence become bodies without organs. That is, they are bodies of work which articulate dis*organ*ization, deterritorializing static modern conceptions of organization (of form, psychology, the self) in favor of different forms, forms which "are an inevitable exercise or experimentation, already accomplished the moment you undertake [them], unaccomplished as long as you don't" (ATP 149). Exercises or experimentations which engage the release of desiring intensities, bodies without organs are a positive exploration of release from habitual behavior patterns imposed on the individual and the text by the State. Released, they are nomadic; always transient, always becoming.

He's not breaking any new ground here. He's writing himself out of a job with this project it's not going to catch anybody's eye. What he knows Nothing he can say in this meeting will surprise Basil or interest him all that much or change his mind about the project. So he doesn't say much. He feels throughout that Basil cares for him. He wonders if Basil is telling him to find a new line of work. He studies Basil's fingernails his face male stern irascible it looks like his father's father and enemy traitor and friend. Walking home he reads Basil's end comments. They say Vex'd pig hymn waltz fuck Bjorsq. Good luck. Basil Utter.

6/19 spends the whole day watching whales on The Nature Channel then on a tape of The Nature Channel and then on a whale video he ordered special who knows when in his Melville phase. He's obsessing has obsessed at least a little over whales because Melville did and that was interesting. And in his books Ron's got a thing for whales there's got to be something to whales then if they both dwell on them he wants to know what that is he wants to get the whale thing. He hasn't gotten it yet in fact watching whales makes him a little anxious wondering why he can't develop his own interests. His are always someone else's first does that make them any less interesting. Maybe it makes them more his working through other people's ideas obsessions gives them an extra dimension. Maybe this is an excuse. Does an obsession with other people's obsessions count as a legitimate obsession he doesn't know the whales look tiny on the screen one color. He feels dry and constipated if you know that feeling it's what he likes to call simulation feeling. Simulation feeling comes from dealing with copies in the absence of originals. Sometimes copies are all we have he figures you make do with what you have. Maybe it would be different if he could reach over the edge of a dinghy off the coast of California lay his hands on the rubbery rough back of a sperm or a blue or even if at just

SeaWorld he could once stroke the smooth snout of a Killer. Unmediated physical sensation he finds his swollen cock in his hand. He puts it away. But he can't put away the whales they're locked into his imagination always in the back of his mind. He wants to feel a special relation to them they seem that unique the spouts if he could really see them would be giant ejaculations of course he knows it's just breathing but it's special breathing the exhalation of the largest living animals at fifteen minute intervals is not just ordinary breathing it's like victory rockets shooting up from floating football fields orgasms in celebration of life by bulk life. He has an audio tape of the eerie ecstasy of whale songs calm throbbing poignant that's the kind of song he wants to sing composing it as he goes a new career on the street corner. Chanting for passersby. He can't sing he's got a terrible voice. But he wants to speak at least or write because he knows we live in intel in words or pictures made from words. It's the water in which we swim. He needs to get at something different disorienting a nonsense of things that's not not but non. Beyond the alphabet surprising. Like Ron. Who is Brillig. Mojo. Maybe one day he's going to spell out a song that will be the key to The Problems a song that did and didn't exist before. The lyrics would be these. Furk jygs vix'd nomph waltz bicz. Nymphs waltz jog fluck vax rod bq. Hymn waltz fuck vex prod big sqj. Hymn waltz fuck sex gip v.d. bjorq. Vex'd nymphs waltz jig fuck borq. He's dizzy not inspired he's catering which he does nights and weekends. He's spreading tablecloths setting silverware the water glass at the tip of the knife the wine glass above the spoon. He's making salads icing glasses pouring water setting butter cream sugar bread. When the guests drift in he drifts out with hors d'oeuvres and they feed frenzy surrounding him picking off one two three hors d'oeuvres not all for them of course but the wife will have one they're grilled tuna chunks on crackers. Gilled chuna trunks for leakers what was that. Haveone NgeelaHavetwo

NgeelaHavethree NgeelaHavefourthey'resmall. Then wine
then salad then wine he's got a glass for himself in the
back room on the job strictly not kosher it's a Bat Mitzvah
supper. The Bat Mitzvah girl's fat and unhappy. Even at
the center of the party she seems friendless. This scene is
all wrong. Hava NgeelaHava NgeelaHava Ngeela Hey Ho
Hum. Then clearing salad then dinner plates servers
snaking out in a production line to cover one table then
the next then the next then the next then the next then
the next then the next then the next then the next then
the next then the next then the next then the next then
the next then the next then the next then the next he's got
a glass for himself in the back room strictly not kosher it's
a Bat Mitzvah supper. Salmon with asparagus and a
special sauce chef's secret he's got a glass for himself in
the back room. Of course he'll get more bread. He looks
like a penguin bow tie black tux shirt black pants shoes
socks sucking a mint. He eats as he works snitching rolls
and hors d'oeuvres. Then the music and flashing lights the
DJs are swarthy skinny they're Italian very fluid vibrating
with the music and coffee it's decaf but whatever they
want it to be he says it is and clearing plates and screaming children thirteen-year-old boys touching fourteen-year-
old girls with big breasts already small breasts high skirts
and smooth smooth legs. He's got a glass for himself in
the back room strictly not kosher smooth legs and firm
asses and sweaty foreheads and clearing dinner plates
dessert's a sweets plate on each table he's got his two and
the waitstaff snaking out again with a cream crepe with
raspberry sauce and whipped cream and then fuck the
guests the waitstaff eats. Not the special sauce they know
what's in it. Na Na nanana Na Na nanana Na Na nanana
ney no nuh. Na Na nanana Na Na nanana Na Na nanana
ney no nuh. Neet neet neetneetneetneet neet neet
neetneet neetneet neet neet neet ney no nuh. Breast plate
please breast breasts tender young breasts with a glass of
wine ice in this one so to not look suspicious like it's

sprite. It makes clearing easy though the plates the cups the glasses the silverware the tablecloths his feet hurt he's fat it's because the whales weren't real and if the whales aren't real what is. It's the wrong scene a negative halluci-nation too much clopclop not enough portholes it's the nowhale feeling so suck ass or jerk anchor leaker. Shoosh Eck.

What's Shoosh Eck.

Ask Ron.

What does he say.

He says Bjorsq.

He says.

>Bjorsqi poppamomma
>Wocky wocky
>Plastic jam
>Iron blintzes
>Fill the inches
>Sooky buby nishtgedeit

What the fuck does that mean.

Figure it out yourself.

Date he can't deny the existence of horrors he sees
them every day. Flashes of them. Their shadows. On tv
mostly on the evening news rape camps villages slaugh-
tered skeletons under drooping sacks of flesh razor wire
molested children bodies dragged dismembered. But they
only emerge like the bright spots on the insides of his
eyelids they're not there when his eyes are open. Still
they're there all the same. They're like a secret code
emerging from the white noise that makes the sense of the
world. They're the nonsense but that doesn't mean they
don't mean something very important. He wants to understand what. It's why he keeps watch he's trying to see
what he can of what he senses is the real reality beyond
the everyday. But or maybe because none of it touches
him he's immune he thinks protected middle class inocu-
lated partly damaged but not dead. He's taken a needle in
the ass to repel pain and death. He thinks though if you
have no pain and no death you have no life. Right. You're
the living dead a walking zombie with a pulse but insen-
sate. So he has urges. Does he want to move over to the
other side to die or go insane. Maybe. Maybe not. What
he does want he thinks is to screw things up. If you screw
things up they fall apart. If things fall apart then you're
under the skin of the world. And when you reemerge
when things come together again they come together

differently. Different than before. So what does this mean it means he wants to fail. Believe it or not. He aspires to failure. It's possible however he realizes to fail at failing. Or to make of it a howling success.

11/01 the student comes in two parts. One part comes on a chair in the front of the room in skirts and low cut blouses. Her hair is curly blond. He doesn't know if it's permed. He knows that she's Midwestern Frankenstein not too big but solid with white skin a little red in her cheeks and when he looks at her he sees northern countries where blood buries itself to escape the cold. He knows she's divorced returning to school. He knows she has a two-year-old daughter it's what she's told him. She's an English major. In class she says smart things but her comments are looped frustrated like she can't clear her head. When he pays attention he sees her watching him while listening to his lecture. Concentrating on him. On him. This shakes him this one student when thirty student heads are most if not all pointed his way. When he pays attention he sees she knows he's noticed her his voice drops beats he loses his sentences. This shakes him more he wants to check his fly. What he's trying to tell them is that the sections of Ron Sukenick's *98.6* portray three different landscapes three different worlds. Perhaps it's best to say that the sections portray three different geographical moments because they don't really show different landscapes cut from different parts of the very same continent or even disparate worlds that might or might not overlap but three different non-synchronous moments that detail the same geography in different ways focusing on pieces of the same picture or formations from the same bedrock. Look at it this way. You've got three transparencies laid on top of each other. Each is one section of 98.6. When the student smiles at him he sees it in his peripheral vision. When she nods still concentrating encouraging or starts to raise her hand or flips her hair he wants to look right at her. He doesn't do it. One transparency outlines a phase of unhappiness is full of a painfully dissatisfying reality. Another outlines a phase of imagination where experimental life is encouraged and reality takes creative turns though he adds they're risky not guaranteed. The final gives us the phase of illumination where ideals are realized idealized worlds exist. He's had students watch him before. While one transparency is on top it predominates and its phase is most evident. But still through the phase on top you can see the other phases below through around it a part of it though less clearly. He's never let it shake him. He's never let himself wonder why he's never let it shake him. The phases are therefore happening simultaneously are different moments or the same story even if one tends to stand out in greater relief. Geographical moments. What he's trying to tell them is something he doesn't understand completely that's why he wants to tell them about it. Non sense a different way of looking at things. So you have different *moments* of the same story happening simultaneously in different ways. A student who doesn't look at him the way The Student does but makes sure to bring herself to his attention she has trouble with the porn. It's how she describes the content of the first section. We might as well be reading Penthouse or Hustler don't you think. What he thinks knows all of a sudden is that he's been approaching the book all wrong at least where teaching goes. The Student comes up after class because she's interested in the idea of geographical moments branching like split time lines in science fiction only the branches don't spread out like roots but are parallel on top of each other while still touching though I guess. She catches him looking down the open neck of her blouse. She blushes. He looks away. After a second her nipples stick through the soft fabric.

Sukenick claims that as a writer of new fiction, he is informed by "a theory of composition" and that he considers "form a dynamic, rather than an inert, element of composition...[that is] not a given but an object of invention, part of content and, like it, determined only in composition" (In Form ix). The dynamic forms generated in composition (not surprisingly what Sukenick calls generative narratives) map the "movement of the mind as it organizes the open field of the text" (In Form 13). Wallace Stevens, of course, figures importantly in these of Sukenick's ideas; it is in his study of Stevens that Sukenick begins to fix upon and develop the Stevensian interest in *reality* as flux, the processes of change in this flux, and the function that imagination plays in making the ego both immanent to this reality and yet also capable of revealing it. For Sukenick, this leads to a position committed to the understanding that *the writer* cannot achieve the ideal of transcendence so important to many modernists, but only be immanent to a chaotic reality: "One cannot have control 'over' that of which one is part, or even formulate it completely—one can only participate more deeply in it" (In Form 4). The writer can only hope to approach the compositional synthesis of consciousness and experience so brilliantly exemplified in the work of Beckett. In approaching this synthesis, "the need both to comprehend and to participate in the flow of life is resolved because writing, as an act, is simultaneously part of life and about it" (In Form 6).[4]

---

[4] **Immanence/Insertions**

The immanence that Sukenick contemplates typically revolves around a cycle of *insertions*. For him, fiction involves an insertion of the writer into life and an insertion of the writer's life into the text. The text is, not surprisingly, at some point inserted into life—the writer's life that is—and in its turn the writer's life becomes the text. Sukenick's relentless awareness of the reality of these insertions and the realities created by these insertions leads to a text/life/writer/text in which each successive *entering into* of different states effectively annihilates the existence of an *outside* state at all and renders ineffective any simple distinctions one might make between what is text and what is context.

11/08 The Student comes in two parts here comes
the second part she falls in love with him. He's married.
It's 1998. She stops talking to him after class starts talking
to him during office hours. First she's got questions about
Sukenick then comments about Sukenick she sits in the
wooden chair by his desk. Then she brings him a latte and
they talk about school which isn't easy school isn't after a
certain point. In life. They decide. Then she sits in the
chair but pulls it around the desk Dom's not there touches
his knee. At one point. To accentuate a comment he
stiffens he moves his knee away. Maybe he's never much
wanted to live in interesting times. Maybe he's lazy. Maybe
he's too smart damn him he's never gone to sea in a small
boat never to the desert the jungle. Maybe he's interested
in the extraordinary but abstractly it gives him a mental
erection. Maybe that's all maybe that's what's wrong.
Because he likes The Student. She's smart. He looks at
The Student's legs her breasts the way her skirt folds in a
small pouch between her legs. When she sits. And her
upper arms and the side of her face her eyes but from the
side and her ear. And he wants to climb in The Student's
bed and into The Student herself. To fuck closing his eyes
he wants to go headfirst between her legs until he's inside
up to her lungs thrashing around half in and out a human
cock. He thinks his head is going to explode. Does she

like him or Ron. She married when she dropped out of school maybe dropped out of school because she married tried to make it work they both worked. The Husband worked for the City the Forestry Department aka he planted trees. She was a waitress an administrative assistant a check-out clerk a masseuse she loved him. She rubbed his back in the evenings free of charge she didn't rub his back after a while he hit her she moved out. The short version. She was pregnant. She's tired. She's got a two-year-old. She's looking for help because she doesn't know where she's headed even now after she's gotten it together is back in school. School supplies a rough approximation of where she might be headed education leads to a career a life etc. But this is only a vague map. She needs more help. He's her teacher. He's not young enough to know nothing. He's not old enough to be out of touch. All he has to do is act and this could become a party of the second part. This party he suspects would be a skid completely out of control it would wreck his life. He wants it the skid he wants her. He wants to find out what an affair with her would mean where it would lead. Because he doesn't know. And this is what stops him. He can't quite imagine all that happens next and no one can imagine it for him he can only do and he's not sure he's ready to act and anyway he's not an actor he's a part of the audience. Isn't he and in the larger scheme it'll all end up the same old story only in a new context how many times has this drama unfolded he's seen it himself any number of times man leaves wife for younger woman etc. Who needs it. He does and this makes him afraid. He finds excuses to miss his office hours.

Many Christmas's[2]   **Agent Fox William**[3]
ago, Frank Costanza Mulder, an Oxford-

went to buy a doll   trained psychologist with
for George. There   a photographic memory,
was only one doll   is one of the FBI Violent
left and when he   Crimes division's best
reached for it,   agents, although he
so did another   is in disfavor with
man. After not only his superiors
So many dangers   struggling but also his
colleagues   for the doll,
because of his interest he
in the Bureau's thought there could
X files. He   be another way. The
stumbled upon these   doll was destroyed,
files, dealing with   but out of that, a
unexplained phenom-   precautions.   new holiday was
ena, during his first   born. It was
three years with the   called Festivus.
Bureau, as a crack   A Festivus for
analyst in the   the rest-iv-us....
Bureau's Festivus Information:
It is not   Celebrated behavioral sciences
enough   December 23rd department. [Chris
each year. The Meal: Carter, *Starlog* #
Whatever you want.   *201*, April 1994]
During the last few   His fascination
weeks in December when   with the para-
Festivus takes place   normal stems
families and friends   BwO.   from a child-
get together at   hood incident—

---

[2] From seinfeld-fan.com, at http://seinfeld.digitalrice.com/html/
festivus.htm.

[3] From the X-Files Frequently Asked Questions, at http://bedlam.rutgers.
edu/x-files/xfilesFAQ.html.

the dinner   his sister Samantha
table and have   disappeared from
something called   their home in
"the Airing of Chilmark, Mass.
Grievances". (pop. 650)
During when
he was this time, we share
12 and she was with family and
8. Mulder claims   friends all the
she was abducted   ways they have
by aliens; during   disappointed us
regressions he   consistency   over the past year.
recalled hearing   After the Airing
his sister's cries   of Grievances,
for help, and a   we get together
bright light which   right in the same
kept him paralyzed night to do something
called "Feats and told him that
of Strength". his sister would
This is where the be all right.
the industrial Shooting in Jonesboro
revolution and its   Arkansas![4] Third School
consequences have   Shooting in 5 months!
been a disaster for   Take   Are they interconnected
the human race. They   to Bill Clintons Birth
have greatly increased   Place. Written by JP
the life-expectancy   Essene Editor What's
of those of us who HOT! In 3/24/98
live in There's a
the   BIZARRE "advanced"   organism
mathmatical connection countries, but

---

[4] Essene, JP. "Shooting in Jonesboro Arkansas! Third School Shooting in 5 months! Are they interconnected to Bill Clintons Birth Place." What's HOT!, 3/24/98: http://www.theeunderground.net/Features/features182 jonesboro.shtm.

to these school they have destabilized
shootings and Bill   society, have made
Clintons birthplace.   life unfulfilling,
When you start to   organization   have subjected human
connet the cities   beings to indignities,
of many recent tragedies,   have led to widespread
all the connections psychological suffering
(in the go through
Third World to Hope Arkansas
physical suffering Clinton's birth place!
as well) and have   The most recent
inflicted severe   school shooting
damage on the   organs   was in Jonesboro,
natural world. The   Arkansas, Bills
continued development   home state!
of technology will worsen   At least 5 are DEAD!
the situation. It   Many are wounded!
will certainly lead The shooters subject
are only human beings to greater
11 and 13!   indignities and inflict
The 11 year   greater damage on the
old was identified   natural world, it
as Andrew Golden and   will probably
the 13 year old as   *Cancerous*   lead to greater
Mitchell Johnson.   *Tissue:*[5]   social disruption and
You heard it here FIRST!   psychological suffering,
The four students   and it may lead to
who were killed increased physical
suffering were Paige Herring,
even in   12, Stephanie Johnson
"advanced"   , 12, Natalie Brooks,

---

[5] Deleuze, Gilles and Félix Guattari. A Thousand Plateaus: Capitalism and Schizophrenia. Translated by Brian Massumi. Minneapolis: University of Minnesota Press, 1993.

countries.
2. The industrial[6]
-technological system
may survive or it may
break down. If it
survives, it MAY
eventually achieve
a low level of physical
and psychological also
suffering, but only
after passing through
a long and very painful

11, and Brittany
Varner, 11,
were killed in
the incident. Later
Tuesday evening, Shannon
Wright, a sixth grade
language and spelling
teacher who was pregnant,
died at St. Bernard's
hospital.   In 5 months
that's 3 school shootings.
The first was in Pearl

[6] Kaczinski, Theodore. "The Unabomber Manifesto."
net.manifesto.unabomber: http://204.156.22.13/message/prophet/
unabomb/part01.htm

4/25 the news tells him to be proud he's not dead. Not not dead by suffocation under a pile of shit in the camp latrine or a tunnel collapsed or in a muddy bog the wrong place to squat for the night. Or dead beaten to death by guards after having been forced to copulate with his daughter after watching his wife gang-raped hanging for months in a bamboo cage dehydrated because what comes in he shits right out. Or dead been thrown out of a helicopter after torture bamboo under his fingernails electrodes on his balls. Or dead his skin toasted off in a napalm attack. Or dead shot down in the desert breathing oil smoke fumes and airborne toxins. Or dead fallen prey to any one of a number of grotesqueries he carries in his memory the vast culture failures of recent generations. So many moments the phenomenon of life energy in the absence of creative forms turning against itself. So many. No. His triumph is that he's not dead or dying from the ubiquitous. The everyday just that. No virus has shut his body down. He's not been exposed that he knows of to chemicals radiation airborne pollutants. His cells don't proliferate unregulated. He's not been cut or shot in a robbery on a highway in the classroom. He's never picked the wrong fight in a bar at a party he doesn't ingest much red meat fatty foods artificial flavors. He doesn't smoke tobacco or dope. Not too much alcohol. Doesn't get too much sun. Filters his water. The doctor's gloved finger finds nothing swollen. He's not been around the diseased. He's not sure what he thinks of health the ideal life in the face of ubiquitous death is everyone's goal it seems. Is that it.

5/09 what The Wife wants she says is a change.
Something. Anything. No not anything. Something. A
change. A specific change.

What he wants to know he says is what that is. What
change. What does she want.

She's not sure she says although she is. Obviously.
Maybe. She's sure she doesn't want new things which she
can have new clothes new furniture new toys a new car
though that would be a stretch.

She says I mean I don't want new clothes.

She says and I don't want new furniture.

She goes through a list one thing at a time.

She says I don't want these things. These are not
what I want.

She says setting her face and I don't want to re-
arrange the furniture which is what he does when the
pages of his dissertation shape themselves into Basil
Utter's face.

She doesn't want new things for the apartment.

She doesn't want a new apartment.

Well what the fuck does she want.

He's not stupid. He knows not to ask. But he does
anyway his stomach is tight enough to shorten his breath
his morning class went badly. He's a boring fat underpaid
lecturer. An overeducated housekeeper live-in cook. He's

a fucking caterer. In every fucking sense. Well what the fuck does she want.

Not to be yelled at first off The Wife yells her face red.

5/09 Transcript Just something.
Something what.
Something different.
Different than what. What makes you so unhappy.
I don't know.
What do you mean you don't know.
I don't know exactly.
But you know. You must know if you want a change.
Don't you know. Don't you want a change.
I don't know. What do you mean.
Jesus. What's wrong with...
     .

     .

Not what's wrong. What's wrong with. With me.
I didn't say that.
But that's what you meant.

     .

That's not what I meant to say.
Not what you meant to say. But what you meant.
No. What I meant is...
What.
Don't you know.
Know. No! What. What the fuck you come in here
and just because you've had a shitty day. Fuck!
     That.

What.
I don't need this.
You don't need What.
How dare you speak to me like that.
What.
I just don't need this.
What.
This.
What. What. What don't you need. You come in here and you *want a change* and you *don't need this*. What.
You obviously feel the same way.

.

.

Maybe I do.
Well then you know.
Maybe I do.
It's not me.
What's not you.
You said you knew.
Maybe I do.
Well it's not me.

.

.

So it's me.
I don't know.
What's me.
I didn't say that.
What.
That it's you.
But that's what you meant.
I don't even know what we're talking about.
Me. You're saying that because of me you can't get what you want.

.

Which is something different.

.

Which is what.

What.

7/03 he feels uneasy. Uneasy and depressed for hours now he's been wandering from room to room trying to shake off this growing dread of what. Of being alone. Yes. No. Of failure. Yes. No. Of change of something different. Yes. No. Of loss. Yes. No. There's nothing to be afraid of he keeps thinking and the scary thing is he believes it he doesn't care enough to be afraid. It makes him want to puke. But then he finds he's afraid again. He tries to think of nonsense life on the rhizome home sweet rhizome himself a big bulging endless tuber with no beginning or end ramified surface extension crabgrass that always cheers him up or at least distracts him but he becomes nauseous again he can't pin down why his dread condenses out of nowhere like a fog like an oppressive neighborhood or cheap furniture or wearing a dead man's clothing. He knows it comes from himself he wants to fend it off he doesn't want to feel it. He doesn't have a choice. He's in it. He's as immanent to it as immanent gets. In this life. This doesn't mean that he can't go up or get out but not right now. He's out of ideas. It's weird but this cheers him up a little he feels like he knows what he's talking about. If he can figure this out then he can figure out more he can write it down convey this feeling to someone else he can succeed in some odd way. He turns around finds anxiety dispelled he blinks and everything is

different that is it's the same but as if he's seeing it from
the other side as if he's passed through a door or a mirror
what seemed the reflection is now the reality or maybe
there are two realities each the reflection of the other and
he's aware of both. Simultaneously. Two moments he can
live in. Two worlds. He feels schizophrenic. He feels tired.
The dread is there again a tide that ebbed then returned
without his noticing. He remembers having double vision
but he doesn't have it anymore he's back in his life and he
wonders why. He's back in his life and after all he's
learned everything is the same as before. He's to blame.
He blames The Wife. It's the world. TV's fault. Basil Utter.
He doesn't know. He doesn't want to think about it.
What's the difference. Maybe it's all out of his control.
What does that mean. He's working in an aircraft factory
assembling DC-3s the 1937 two motored first modern all
aluminum airliner they still make them. This boy is going
to put one together in thirty minutes says Mussolini strut-
ting down the assembly line with a group of Nazi VIPs.
How am I going to do that he thinks needless to say very
uptight he knows the consequences if he doesn't do it that
is he doesn't know them exactly but he knows they will
be so unimaginably severe that he doesn't even imagine
not doing it. Someone should tell him how to do it. He
needs a book. A guide book. That's what he needs.
Sukenick not Sukenick. Sukenick will gladly tell him how
to live you make it up as you go along. It's just that easy.
Improvise. Because how you live determines what life is
at least for the moment. Right. Boiled down catchphrases
sometimes it's all you can work with it's not enough. Life's
not a wholly subjective enterprise they both know it and if
you find yourself tied to the wrong port you're pretty well
screwed. Who but the crazy and stupid would ignore
brute reality. He's finding he can't.

What.

You think it's easy.

5/24 it had never been easy between them. Two people meet and though they're not sure they like each other it seems as if they might start dating. They're suited in some ways by interests temperaments similarities of all sorts and they do. Date. The Dates are awkward at first uncomfortable but this doesn't deter them enough who knows why no other options immediately at hand or a sense of something bigger coming. They keep dating. They've both had one relationship bad enough that they're jaded just a little in the long run they don't so much fall in love as they step into it gradually all the way measuring each other's pros and cons. Against their expectations of a partner. In the end or the beginning that is of their lives together they're fully rationally prepared for what marriage will likely bring ups and downs positives and negatives satisfactions and disappointments etc. What is this. A late twentieth-century anti-romance. An exceedingly dispirited memory of a doomed relationship. Is it too negative a picture. What really do they like about each other. Where are the happy moments in the sketch alluded to but hardly described. Earlier toward the end of college he'd fallen into a something like nothing he'd ever believed could be it had been like love made flesh real actual alive. When he and she were together almost always they couldn't bear to be apart they radiated an air of enchantment connection an absolute unending interest and understanding for each other an overwhelming intoxicating irresistible desire to touch and hold and orbit the other's body hands hair shoulders legs feet stomach ears and backs. Their fascination with each other was magnetic and mindless. In bed in the woods on the beach in cars in bathrooms the kitchen they fucked with a brainless energy that contorted them again and again into all couplings short of swapping skins. What he wanted eventually was to smash her head into pudding. She thought he was stifling she fucked someone else. He screamed at her. She tried to run him over with her car. It all felt so real. You'd think he would have known better handled things better not gotten so screwed up made such a mess. What a fucking miserable mess that was. He thought he'd kill himself. Is there such a thing as knowing better. Is one way of being screwed up better or worse than another. He wishes she'd run him over would run him over now it would feel better than feeling nothing at all. Which is where he is in part or where he's headed in full. That's a question.

2/15 the apartment's chilly. His toes his nose one arm they're all cold even under the covers. He doesn't remember the alarm he turned it off maybe never turned it on. The Wife's not here. He doesn't remember. Her leaving. He rolls onto his back stares at the ceiling. It's lime green. It's cracked bucked peeling. He wonders how many layers of paint it's seen how much spackle wonders why it doesn't leak it's right under the roof the top of the building he doesn't get up. Doesn't get up he tells himself he can't get up if he can't get it up. Wills his cock to rise. He thinks of his students so young most of them he thinks of The Student of her ass in her jeans what her ass would look like without jeans on the bed on her knees her elbows her legs spread her ass staring at him her tits hanging touching the bed her arms her head turned back looking for him waiting for him thinks of putting his hands on her ass his arms around her ass palms on her stomach of thrusting in first she's so slick so wet then before she realizes into the eye winking at him boring in he's not hard she's not there he hates himself he knows he shouldn't. Shouldn't. Fuck it. Why bother. He reaches to the floor feels around finds the remote. Turns on the tv. Andy Griffith. Whatever happened to his wife. Why not marry Helen Crump. Opie should be less well adjusted than he is really. He hates the Andy Taylor character the paternalism the knowitallness the early episodes at least. He doesn't change the channel. He's not going to get up. He's going to watch Andy Griffith in two lives he'll wait through two episodes of The Andy Griffith Show and then watch Matlock it's right after for an hour. He wonders why the first show was named after the actor the second the character he wonders who Andy Griffith thinks he really is he wonders what his friends think of him. He's not hungry. He's not going to get up. He's not going to class. His hands are swollen red dry cracked pimply oozing. They itch. He's got eczema allergies his hands touch anything and they're ground chuck. It comes it goes it's been here for weeks he can't hold a pen without pain he can't type he can't wash dishes he's useless. It's nerves. It's his immune system. It's not a fungus not sebhorreia not psoriasis the doctors don't know what it is they call it eczema. They're sick of him his incurable problems. His family doctor's getting divorced has his own worries depression doesn't care. He doesn't care. He's not going to die he doesn't feel much like living. He's thirty-something. He's never going to have kids. He's never going to get the job he wanted all he ever wanted to do really tenure-line faculty Porfessor. He knows without thinking about it things aren't going to work out the way he wanted them to not for lack of trying. He can't rationalize it away. This fact. He tries. He tells himself he'll do something else head in another direction he'll find it satisfying that's life. Don't give up make it meaningful whatever it is. He knows what he needs to do. Try to make it happen give it his best shot figure it out get going the Frankenstein way the manifesto of the middle-class people working hard. Not really getting ahead not admitting they're not moving anywhere. Fuck. Nothing's going to change his problem. He's not going to get what he wants what he's worked hard for he's not asking for charity to win the lottery for a life of leisure. What he wants is to work underpaid underrespected the rest of his life teaching twenty year olds four classes a term a small school no time for research. It's hard crappy frustrating it's all he wants. It's not going to happen. For him for seventy percent of people like him. He's married his in-laws don't get along they can't change it's too late. His hands hurt. It's hopeless this isn't him quit whining.

But if not that then what.

12/28 imagine. Imagine an unreasonably large house Victorian with three floors and a basement hardwood floors throughout. It's old but immaculately restored. It's beyond his means but this somehow doesn't matter it's all his and his wife's they have one child they're thinking about another. They'll do a lot of thinking it's not a decision that can be made lightly. In the long run all deliberations will be beside the point and they'll then have one boy and one girl. How can they know this it's written in the stars. How can this be he doesn't ask he just accepts it. In the same way that they have and will always have the same group of loyal friends who whatever ups and downs will always be the people to whom they'll turn again and again and again week after week for companionship and fun and guidance and solace and whatever else is necessary in the face of the conflicts in their lives. This reassures him it feels right there's a pattern here as in their group two married couples and three singles one single man and two single women a total three men and four women himself and The Wife included it's a nice balance. He turns to the men when necessary when The Wife can't satisfy his needs. She turns to the women when he can't help her it always works out well or at least well enough that whatever happens in their world is interesting but not catastrophic. He just can't understand how he affords all this the house his expensive antique Volvo it looks like a Porsche. These are not the trappings of a professor he's not a professor but a businessman what else could he be doing he's in advertising. It's a creative enough enterprise while still lucrative he dreams in his spare time of being a writer. He takes an evening writing class where he's tutored with great care by of all things a published novelist. Above all he has hope he's a thoughtful and steady man. And curiously good looking trim and built The Wife has the understated but strikingly beautiful appearance of a tv star. They still after who knows how many years of marriage make passionate love. He's been drawn once as has she to others flirted with the possibility of an affair but these were merely predictable blips in the course of a marriage. Who hasn't experienced them they came to they'll always come to naught. This much is obvious. As is the fact that whatever the specifics of the next thirty or so years of their lives they'll still be together growing old together safe and sound this is the bigger picture. Happiness ever after and so on this is not wholly implausible. If it were someone would say something. Right. Wouldn't they it's not all in his head is it. This is the real story. Get it.

8/25 he finds himself floating in coastal waters with six other survivors. Their raft keeps them afloat but he's worried that when they hit land they'll drift apart. He guides the raft this way and that trying to maneuver into the harbormouth waving and shouting at nearby ships. Over here this way help us meantime enjoying everyone's attention and then they too start to shout for help. They built the raft when they'd heard news of the storm figured it would flood their huts and carry them out to sea and then maybe back to land. Inhabited land. When a ship breaks water like a wet cliff next to them they're taken aboard. He loses sight of everyone but the Skipper. They're not much suited to normal life normal jobs back in the world so they seek each other out. For company. Nostalgia. Reminiscences. They miss each other. Their lives together. They seem out of context when they're not out to sea they have now a kind of closure but it's all wrong. They miss each other. Their lives together. And he's being hunted by two clumsy spies hunted for some-thing he has something wildly top secret and there are then plot twists galore. Then something. Then something else. Then they take a nostalgia tour out to sea it's for the heck of it. A storm hits out of nowhere. He's ruined the compass. Somehow. They don't know where they are. A shadow solidifies in the mist. The beach perfect in size

and shape a half moon with white white sand. The sloop
tacks struggling into the harbormouth wallowing in the
swell a jagged open wound on its front port side. Skipper
sends them up the bay on a close beat bow bobbing
through the chop while he hauls in sail slicker shining. It's
just dawn. They're struggling into the island. Skipper
grounds onto the beach heads up as he drops the main
halyard Skipper handles the jibsheet as they come about.
He topples over the side of the boat lithe like a monkey
one arm clutching the rail. His body extends far enough
so he can drop. Skipper throws the anchor his way he
pulls it far up along the beach.

We made it he says.

But where says Skipper.

He kicks something at his feet an old sign a plaque
of some sort he bends down picks it up.

What's that.

A sign he says.

Well what does the sign say says Skipper.

He brushes it off his eyes widen he pauses.

Well says Skipper what does it say.

Everyone's topside now he holds it up for them to
see.

It says Vex'd pig hymn waltz fuck bjorsq.

He doesn't know where that is.

The Children of Frankenstein

The ocean hunches its shoulder and throws itself against the cliffs. A pause and the wave explodes against the rocks jets of foam shoot into the air high as the overhanging cliff. Hang there an instant as auroras of spray fall back to the surf. Glittering in the sun. A second later the wave gathers itself over the shining wet sand of the cove skips a beat and slams down on the beach. The waves aren't especially big the ocean isn't even trying. Its strength is implied in its calm. The surf sounds like a passing locomotive. Its strength is implied in the deliberation of its pausings. It rumbles out like a freight train. A small part of the picture a red car winds along the ocean-side highway. A helicopter rainbow-colored buzzes the surf.

They don't live anywhere near the surf unless a mile off a Great Lake counts. Most of them have never heard real surf pumping like blood through their veins. They're fascinated by it though or at least Matt is watching tv

Magnum P.I. Hawaii Five-O even Baywatch. Sometimes he seems to go on and on in the pause in his day between writing teaching reading hung in suspension his eyes on the screen in the blank between as when you stop thinking with your brain's right side and suddenly hours have passed. Then something breaks in. Maybe it's only the way Bud will suddenly come in the front room to watch too. The way August will stop what she's doing to come in and make an arch comment a critique an observation about the show. Or something else breaks in. And Matt begins to really see and hear what's in front of him in a way begins to think and talk about it it becomes important a measure a part vital to his reality. And at the same time ridiculous in a way. Why. The tv sky an unreal blue electronic always worse on their old set red cars too red a digital palette the tall pines jagged to the edge of the ocean cliffs their green flat against the blue of the sky. The 'copter dodges along the edge of the surf like a halfback cutting through the line. Women with huge breasts dance back and forth in the surf. It's all exciting and beautiful and he'd like to be there but it's not the real thing. What's that. Gee Matt thinks life is strange even in the everyday the things everyone does without even thinking unreal. But cool. He couldn't live without what's in front of him right now he tries to think about the feeling rising in his stomach a tightening his mind focuses but gets absorbed in the show the plot the charac-ters good or not. After a while stunned beyond thought he drifts up the stairs to the bathroom.

Downstairs the rooms don't get much light. Not like the basement which is dark and cool on the sunniest days

two casement windows the only links outside. But not as
much light as they could with the hedges growing in front
of the windows filtering day and the building next door
cutting off all but sharpest angles of the sun. Because of
this the tv room the kitchen the half-bath and Matt's
bedroom feel muted half-toned calm monochromatic in a
good way. Or at least this is how Matt thinks of them is
why he chose the bedroom he did. He likes subterranean
that's not quite subterranean cavelike but not dark not
dank. He likes being near the tv room too close enough
that he gets dibs on the tube when he wants or needs. He
likes being able to hear a tv hum even if he's not the one
watching. When he lived by himself he ran the tv whenever he was home even if he wasn't watching. It made
him feel less alone it still does. He knows this was is
ridiculous he's not alone now really but he doesn't care.
This is how he feels and he knows how he feels and this
is how he acts on feeling and knowing. This is no mindless compulsion. He heads up the stairs to the shower past
August's room which she shares with Bud their parents
were hippies that's why the names. Past Gillian's room
which she shares with Matt the other Matt who's short and
dark like himself. At the end of the hallway next to the
bathroom Mel's door is open she's sitting in bed reading
next to Ron who's still asleep. She smiles and nods. She's
reading Wittgenstein Matt sees Mel never stops working
reading writing although the way she approaches it it
doesn't seem like she works so much as work is what she
is does in which she finds meaning. Or makes it. What's
the difference. So it's not work with Mel as much as it's
just Mel along with her tomboy prettiness her short hair
her stretched body is almost if not quite awkward. Matt
thinks she must have been an overachiever as a child
encouraged by her parents to be always doing not that
idle hands are the devil's workshop but that doing is
where you find meaning you make it happen. Matt thinks
Mel's parents must have been hippies like August's and

Bud's but a different breed of hippies. He's not sure what
this means a different breed but he's sure that if he tried
to articulate the difference even in his mind it would come
out his mouth at some point and hurt someone's feelings.
They don't talk about their parents anyway not that they
have anything to hide they just don't want to admit they're
still children. He waves a little wave one hand holding his
towel up. He's always been a little in love with Mel. He
hears music from Cam's attic bedroom.

The Mansion was his idea though the name wasn't.
Just across the tracks it's alongside the wrong side of the
river three miles from the U an easy drive or bus ride or
bike ride but a longer walk. So fewer students. Cheaper
prices. It's a fixer-upper for homebuyers a slum if rented it
had been beautiful in better times three floors and four
bedrooms an enormous living room and porches or
balconies off every window and every door and an attic
that's a ballroom-sized bedroom. Now. He'd found it then
he'd found people to live in it asking first friends then
acquaintances everyone in the graduate program with him
at the U. He'd posted a plea to the grad student discussion
list inviting any and all takers to join their group in a
house all their own communal living with privacy also. If
that's what you want. Bud and August liked the price. Mel
and Ron liked the idea of company all hours of the day
and night they like stimulation. Gillian and Matt needed a
place. Cam didn't like the numbers too many people but
he wanted the attic. They all liked that the landlord was
absentee it would make it hard to get things fixed appli-
ances plumbing leaks cracking plaster jammed windows

broken panes but they would have their run of the place decorating painting whatever they wanted. A garden in the backyard. Only Bud suspected that for Matt The Mansion is a Sukenick trip. But Bud doesn't know much about Sukenick really just enough to know that The Mansion their living situation is like something from his books. About Matt Bud doesn't know all that much either if he did he'd know that Matt's got problems. Matt's dissertation is stalled it's supposed to be a critical study of Sukenick an analysis of his theories a study of his fictions something that will situate Sukenick in his cultural moment. It's not happening the dissertation and Matt can't say why. But what he can say about himself is he's not a quitter if one thing doesn't work you try another. So Matt is writing another book he has a novel idea an idea for a novel maybe it will end up helping him write his dissertation maybe it'll end up being his dissertation. In any case Matt thinks he can understand Sukenick by writing a novel recording whatever happens to their group they're all characters in his novel including himself this is what Sukenick would say to do. Or it's what Ron says in *98.6*. Only Bud doesn't want his life to be a novel when Matt suggested they call their home The Monster Bud figured Matt had an agenda insisted on irony. Sure it's a monster but who needs the literal. Let's call it The Mansion.

Once they get started on The Mansion it changes overnight. It still has its problems the cracking plaster broken window weights scratched floors leaking faucets everything that can be wrong with a home is wrong with this one but this doesn't bother them. They make things from flaws. Case in point the windows missing cords tied to weights which will keep them open don't stay open. Nobody can fix the cords it means tearing the window frame apart just to fix a rope impossible. So Mel makes custom window-holder-openers she calls them promising to come up with a better title pieces of broom stick handle sawed up to just the right height for propping. There's a little ball of wood on every tip a different face painted on each. She declines to say if the faces are abstract representations of Matt Gillian Ron Cam Bud August Matt herself but August suspects this is the case. She likes the idea. In the tv room Matt doesn't sand smooth or plaster the cracking bucking walls he gets six cans of paint different colors at a discount. They're cheap because they're weird lime rust canary orange tan robin's blue and he paints onto the sides of every plaster mogul a different color lines every split plaster valley with a different color every rare flat space gets another. When he's done Ron says it looks like a puked-on moonscape but agrees that it's got charm. Bud decides to do the bathrooms the same way. Gillian volunteers for curtain duty she buys two dozen shirts fifties tacky the best kind and cuts them up into strips squares circles triangles. Then she sews them together into rough curtain shapes schizophrenic collages of plaid polka dot striped window-covering polyester and cotton. To the tops of some windows she attaches leftover collars. She attaches one set outside above The Mansion's front door. She proposes they change The Mansion's name to Mr. Mansion but recants in favor of gender neutrality. For lining the cupboards Ron goes to the public library collects every author he can't tolerate Danielle Steel John Grisham Robert James Waller and copies their pages at a nickel a shot. The copies get taped to the bottoms of the warping wood shelves in the kitchen cabinets. The Waller he uses in part for the shelves and part he reserves Ron says he might get a bird and birdcages need lining too. August takes a more experimental approach decides that

the sound of wind chimes might distract from leaking
dripping faucets and so this is what she does. She collects
cans and cuts them up her fingers too but she's stoic
about it little pieces of jangling metal that she strings on
cords and hangs outside all the windows. Matt spends his
time in the basement. He promises something big. Cam
spends his time in the attic. He's cooking up a surprise he
says.

They're all of them even the oldest still good kids of
the middle class Matt says. Some lower-middle some
middle-middle some even upper-middle but all middle
class of one shape or another. Translate. They know the
rules. First rule Bud says Have tolerance if not always true
respect for others' rights. August says Second. Be conscious of your behavior. Where politeness is called for be
polite. Where courteousness is the same. Third Ron. Don't
display publicly your emotions your body your body with
another's body your prejudices. Matt's got Four. Never
discuss money ever. Fifth Gillian shouts. Hygiene must
meet certain standards. Bathe every day. Teeth brushed
morning and evening. The excessive use of cologne or
makeup is forbidden. Sixth Cam. Feel insecure about your
ability to satisfactorily meet these requirements. Seven
addendum says Mel. Find fart and other scatological
humor completely hilarious since other taboo subjects are
not even marginally appropriate and therefore not funny.
Eight says Ron postscript. Find your parents utterly dislik-
able. Make them the villains in every story of injustice and
betrayal and disappointment you've ever experienced. Do
this while subtly indicating that of course you love them

and suffer their flaws. If necessary accept from them cash and other gifts. Be fully aware that doing so bestows upon them power in your relationship insistently deny that doing so bestows upon them power in your relationship. Circumstantial difference in our cases says Matt. They're all of them even the oldest still good graduate students. Intellectuals sort of. They know the rules but don't believe the rules. They're just codes. But they don't rebel against the rules mostly. What they do is self-consciously discuss as a theoretical issue the implications of these rules in a larger Frankensteinian society. What does this mean. Who are they. What's their story.

They live within reach of the world but not quite in it. They've had the usual experiences but they've chosen to withdraw for a while quitting their nine-to-five jobs their benefits plans their accumulation of property a car a house skis a boat. They've moved across the country and set up here. They're not interested in Frankenstein except as a topic of discussion. They want to devote themselves to learning to be around others who want the same. They figure ahead of time they'll study for five to seven years whether they end up degreed or not. They'll all be a minimum of thirtysomething by the time they're through. Some of them have savings most have some university funding. Matt and Bud and Gillian and August work odd jobs too waiting tables handywork for local homeowners. They all rely on their parents when the going gets hard when they need a plane ticket home a new computer money for the dentist. They don't admit to relying on their parents or do it unless they're desperate. It reminds them of something just what they're not sure. They don't think or talk about their past lives these just aren't relevant. They don't worry overmuch about the future though there are no jobs at least as professors anymore anywhere. They live in the moment. This is what they do. They take seminars they read they argue. They go out drinking they blow dope they write they spend semesters reading for prelims and write dissertations for hours a day. They teach they complain complain complain about their students. They grade papers. They bitch about professors and love them the professors in a way beyond complaints. They send out articles they gossip though not too much. They turn into couples and into singles again and couples and again they stay up late get up early play on their computers attend department functions. They go to coffee houses sit for hours suffer and hate school without restraint. They think of quitting they suffer through they go through it and wouldn't be doing anything else. It's difficult demanding satisfying and personal in a way nothing has ever before been for them. Now they have each other and they have The Mansion. This is the most meaningful time they'll any of them ever experience. This is what Matt thinks. He already misses it and it's not over yet.

Let's call it The Big Depression. Let's say that Frankenstein never recovered from The Big Depression. It was such a trauma to our ancestors that it got into their bloodstream their genes. And it got into our parents despite their rebellion there was still that despair all but the best gave up sold out caved into Frankenstein. Even the best who didn't break the lucky smart persistent ones don't

have much to offer us now thinks Matt because it's all
they can do to themselves stay afloat. They offer understanding but mostly it's you've got to do this life by your-
selves. And that's what we do is what Matt suspects we do
it by ourselves. For ourselves. The Big Depression was the
kind of trauma that can only happen when you wake up
from a dream you think is the real thing and it happened
when Frankenstein woke up from the dream of Frankenstein. And it's passed in the genes of the parents to the
hearts of the children. What can you do in the face of that.
Don't dream. Or dream very little is what they do and they
live on very little. They've got a high threshold for tolerance. Bullshit. Everyone Matt knows is pissed off. They're
not getting what they deserve what they want. What is
that. They're not sure. The Big Depression. Joy doesn't get
rid of it. Dope doesn't get rid of it. Sex doesn't get rid of
it. Freedom doesn't get rid of it. Thinking doesn't get rid
of it. Ignoring it doesn't get rid of it. Give up and die.
Emptiness is the best you can hope for. The pause between the beats the clean slate the blank space. Maybe a
little of this Matt thinks. What else.

They can afford it The Mansion's a deal really because it's in a bad neighborhood. Not bad bad people shot
on the street prostitutes in front of the house drug dealers
on the corner. But not good winos sleeping in the alley
gunshots sounding not so far off prostitutes drug dealers
muggers a few streets down. But they have a fence
around the yard and a yard too afterall and the nearby
river's not so accessible that it attracts vagrants. But still.
One afternoon they come home Ron Bud August Gillian

and a neighbor looks up walks across his yard. Takes off his sunglasses. He's in jeans boots his t-shirt reads IF GOD DIDNT WANT MAN TO EAT PUSSY.

You all just move in.

Yes says Bud. This month.

All of you.

Yes. And a few others.

Big place.

Huge Gillian says. It's why we rented it.

Buncha kids in there before you.

Kids how Ron asks.

Kids he says. Looked like they were fifteen. Rode skateboards. Played music.

Students asks Ron.

I never asked em.

You students he asks.

Yes.

You look older than those kids.

We're older students August says smiling. The neighbor ignores her.

My name's Terry he says. I'm your neighbor.

Hi they say. Bud Ron August Gillian.

August he says. That's a weird one. Parents named you after a month.

Them kids forgot to lock their doors. They got scared after someone ripped 'em off.

Ron says Thanks for the tip.

Never know who's checking you out he says.

Right says Bud.

The neighbor nods turns walks across his yard squats next to half a motorcycle takes a part in his hands. The back of his t-shirt reads HE WOULDNT OF MADE IT LOOK LIKE A TACO.

Neighborhood kids sit on the curb in front of The Mansion when they think nobody's home. Or that's what it seems like to Cam who only sees them when the house is empty except for him upstairs in his attic and he looks out and there they are. He can't tell if it's the same kids every time but it's always about the same number five or six about twelve or thirteen years old black kids mostly although sometimes there's a white face in the group. Usually they sit tossing pebbles at cans signs electric poles. Sometimes they won't sit but step down from the curb around each other in a dance their voices going up and down in a kind of song. Sometimes they'll all be in motion. Sometimes they'll dance around one kid. To Cam they seem like little boys. That's all. He was the same when he was a kid hung out goofed off when he got the chance to be around other kids during the school year when he got bussed in from his house in the country. Just kids. Then he'll think they're looking at The Mansion while pretending not to looking out of the corners of their eyes their heads swiveling for a second so they can check things out. Then it's like they were never looking at all and Cam imagines he's imagining things. Or maybe they were taking a peek at the wind chimes. Or there's a squirrel on the roof. On occasion he'll throw open a window or close one if they're all open. The kids never look when he does this. But they never stay long after the noise. After a few minutes they move synchronized off the curb and down the street to the dead end toward the river. Then they disappear. One day when they move off Cam sits watches waits stares. When they pull up a canopy of leaves and slide behind it one second single file and the next nobody there he knows they have a path to the river. They're the only ones who know about it. Now he does too.

What Cam's got going in the attic he shows everyone on a Sunday evening they're all around getting ready for the week it's a stage. Of sorts. But they don't see it right away. What they see is a sheet hanging from the roof sectioning off one end of the room. This is obviously what they're supposed to see or hiding rather what they're supposed to see the rest of the room is just a room bed table tv dresser there's an iron bar jerry-rigged to the ceiling swinging down with clothes hung on it. There's clearly more to see behind the curtain. August says something about curtain number one. Ron wants to know why no curtains two and three. Cam stands not smiling. Cam never smiles or almost never it's a concentration thing not unfriendliness. He's waiting for everyone before leading them behind the sheet. Matt and Mel and Bud are still downstairs. Matt's impatient. He yells downstairs says the fun can't start till everyone's up. Like Christmas morning. So chop chop. This gets them moving first Bud's head at the attic door then all of Bud a tight fit six and some feet in the narrow stairs then Mel with Matt a minute later. They're there but still lost in conversation. Gillian shushes them. Cam waits another half a minute and then says I don't want to be melodramatic he says but what we have here whether you realize it or not is a unique situation. In The Mansion I mean. All of us are together here in a way we'll not likely ever be together again with anyone. As a group. What I'm trying to say he says is that it's not often that you get to live in close quarters with a lot of different people and creative energies. Together living together working together. Cam gets a funny look on his face he stops talking. He's worried he's blowing it he can't get across what he wants to say. August says I know what you mean this helps him. Bud nods and Matt nods and Ron and Gillian and Matt says I agree though really Matt's thinking he's not sure at least not yet if what Cam's describing is so simply a good thing but. He's not going to say this he nods along and this helps Cam. Cam knows they don't understand but they maybe get the drift. Mel's impatient she's never been much for people who can't articulate their thoughts but. She's being too hard on him he must feel on the spot Mel says she just wants to know what's behind the curtain. When Cam doesn't say anything she says Cam you're killing us. What's the surprise. A cam he says and steps to the curtain pulls it aside invites everyone back. A live cam.

What it is is Cam's computer on a computer trolley against one wall with three chairs near it and a ragged plaid loveseat on the wall opposite. Two more white sheets hang one behind the computer one behind the sofa. The final wall opens onto a window covered by a shade. They crowd in they have to the space isn't more than eight by eight feet Bud stands in the middle so he doesn't have to stoop where the roof pitches down in an A. The little white ball on top of the computer Cam says is a Color QuickCam a digital camera. For video and still pictures you can store on the computer. Which can be transmitted over the internet he says. A lot of people do it. He says. Offer images of their worlds themselves share snapped shots with anyone who's interested in looking. Transmit their lives over the internet. I thought we could too. If you want.

What everyone says is this.

.

Then Matt says Like Jennycam. Gillian scrunches her face what August wants to know is huh.

We turn the cam on Cam says. We set it to take pictures every minute or thirty seconds or whatever. We send them to our homepage. He holds his index finger up places it across his lips touches it to the base of his nose. We ask other sites to feature our homepage. Sites like the Nose's HomeCAM's page he says. VoyeurTV. The Voyeurweb. They get a lot of visitors. He touches the mouse kills the screensaver a new screen pops up. He turns on the cam. He waits then on the screen is a picture. It's Cam Bud Gillian August Matt Ron Matt Mel against a backdrop of white there are chairs beside them a ratty brown loveseat in the back there's a wall with a window it's covered by a shade. Weird Matt says. There's no sound Cam says just image. Mel looks at Ron. Bud looks constipated. Ron poses pretending to stick one finger up his nose one hand apelike scratching the top of his head. Gillian looks at Cam looks at Matt says weird is right she looks at the ceiling. August steps behind Bud. Matt puts his arm around Matt and smiles broadly at the camera. Matt smiles too. Cam watches them. After a few five ten fifteen seconds the screen refreshes. It's them again as they are now. Look Ron says we're virtually real. The story of my life Gillian says. Cam points to the print at the top of the screen. I thought we could call ourselves The Children of Frankenstein. He looks at Matt. Matt wonders why Cam has read Sukenick's *98.6*. He wonders what Cam is thinking.

One thing Cam thinks is they should look here he uses the mouse maximizes an application it's the one he used to create their webpage. In it a template is open it's the template for the Children page. In a spot next to their picture there's a scrollable space for text. Cam clicks away from this clicks into his word processor highlights a chunk of text copies clicks back into the template and into the scrollable space for text. He pastes. Saves. Then back to his browser he refreshes. Suddenly with the photo there's narrative.

This morning The Mansion was quiet until around nine. Then all of a sudden everyone was awake. The kitchen sink was running. Coffee was brewing. The toilet was flushing. Doors were opening and closing, and I could hear ——'s voice right through walls and ceilings and floors. It felt unusual, as if in waking up together, everyone in The Mansion was and is operating according to the same biological schedule. Like we're sharing bio-rhythms. Maybe this means we're charmed. Maybe it has something to do with astrological configurations Cam believes in astrology as much as he believes in anything Tarot cards horoscopes fortune tellers mystics. They all offer ways of thinking seeing interpreting experiences they're all useful if you find them useful Cam thinks if they help a person function think see interpret his experiences or hers in useful ways. Or at least interesting ones. And they all get at the truth as far as he's concerned because interpretations don't discover the truth they make it happen they pattern the world. If for example your horo-scope tells you you're going to have a productive day and you believe it and you make it happen then the horo-scope was spot on. Wasn't it.

As you can see we can have a story on our page Cam says next to the photo. You type or paste in what you want here he points like I did. Then save when you're done it shows up there he points. Next to the picture.

Cool Matt says he looks around.

What Mel says is I don't get it. The picture on the screen changes. In it Mel is talking she's got an arm raised at its end the fingers of her hand are curled her index finger half pointing. At the camera. So this thing is always on she asks is this the only camera she asks are you saying you don't care if we come up here into your room and play with your computer.

Gillian asks is this the only camera that's what Gillian wants to know. What she says to Mel is I've got this feeling there are cameras hidden behind the toilets she pretends she's kidding but.

Visual images computer screens don't bother August what she worries about is text. She's not sure about having someone everyone talking about her them on the world wide web. Who would be looking at this is what she wants to know.

About this Matt's got two cents he says I don't think the most savory characters visit these things he says the livecams I've seen are about voyeurism about staring at naked women. He smiles it's how he covers his embarrassment. He turns his face away. Point being if he can comment on livecams he's visited them he's himself not a terribly savory character. Said point is not lost on Mel she gives him a strange look. Then it's not lost on any of them Ron laughs but just a little then Gillian then Bud they both laugh.

I mean I see how this could be fun August says to Bud he looks unhappy. It would be a kick she says to put on some kind of performance we could pantomime our favorite dramatic scenes.

Yeah is what Matt says. What he shouts is STELLA dropping to one knee he clutches his head everyone jumps. This in a few seconds is what they see on the screen everyone staring at Matt on one knee clutching his head.

Or we could dress up as fish and wander around in front of the aquarium August says and create our own livecam screensaver aquarium.

Dress up like fish Bud says.
Well Cam asks Mel. Well.

Well Cam says watching everyone it could be on all
the time but it doesn't have to be. This is the only camera
he says he points and this is the only machine from which
the page transmits. You're welcome to come up here just
keep the sheets pulled. He says it seems like something
he doesn't think needs saying I'm hoping you won't come
up in the middle of the night. Or at inopportune moments.
And Cam says when I write anything on here I plan to
leave off people's names as I've already done. I want to
respect everybody's privacy I expect you'll do the same.
I'll refresh the page to zero every twenty four hours Cam
says the text and the picture if nobody adds to the livecam
on a given day the text box will go blank he says and the
picture will revert to whatever photo we want. He clicks
on a link shows them a picture it's Cam Bud Gillian
August Matt Ron Matt Mel against a backdrop of white
there are chairs beside them a ratty brown loveseat in the
back a wall with a window. Cam says I want a daily
refresh as an interstice. Things can stay on the page for a
little while he says but I don't want anything to stay on
too long an unchanging moment the suggestion that time
has completely stopped. He says I hate it when people
don't update their pages.

Matt agrees he thinks Cam's complaint is legitimate
his solution sound.

In the basement Matt's got four hundred dollars of hydroponics equipment high watt bulbs drainage tanks a filtration system. Since it's show and tell Sunday he thinks he should give everyone his tour he takes them downstairs and downstairs again and again downstairs until they're crowded under the house. There's no sheet no stage no display. Nothing's set up yet but he points out boxes explains what's inside shows them where he'll assemble things. This is in the back of the basement behind discarded wood doors pipes a rusting washtub. He's cleared out a spot that's six by ten. The lights will get hung on pulleys he'll keep them low at first and raise them as the plants grow. The plants he'll put in a bed of artificial rock very porous and under the bed a pump will supply water in and out several times a day. The water he'll saturate with high-power nutrient rich fertilizer there's bat-shit in it he says. It's a controlled environment he says to Ron who points out what they're all thinking. They already have a garden at least have started a garden in the backyard. But you can't grow things in the backyard in the winter Matt says he figures winter is when they'll start to use the rig in three months they'll be able to grow eggplants asparagus artichokes exotic flowers. We can control the nutrients. We can keep the lights on 24/7 he says. Things will grow fast. We can have a garden year round. He says. And we can grow some killer dope Bud says it's what everybody's thinking. When does the fake wall go up Bud asks he doesn't sound like he's kidding. Well we can grow that too if we want Matt says we can all decide what we want to grow rotate crops have all sorts of different stuff all the time. Bud wants to know how much it costs to run high watt bulbs 24/7. It's negligible is what Matt says split eight ways maybe five dollars a person per month. The cost is in the equipment he says and he's always wanted it. Anyway. He's just never had the space before.

Um.

August doesn't mind having a little dope in her possession but she's uneasy about the idea of growing it. What she says is that one corner of this garden should always be morning glories. Ron thinks there could be some serious money made by growing pot though with serious money comes serious risk he's not willing to take he looks at Mel and says he likes fresh tomatoes they'd make a good winter crop. Gillian wants to know if watermelons would be too big to grow she's looking fiercely at Matt meaning she doesn't want pot growing in her basement he'd better somebody'd better say something.

Matt says to Matt I don't think we should grow any pot down here Gillian takes his hand. We've all got too much to lose if we get caught he says he looks around he doesn't think anyone disagrees. And now that we all know this equipment is down here I think we'd all be culpable.

That's fine Matt says like I said it's just one of the things we could grow. So we won't grow it he says what he thinks is he shouldn't have brought everyone down here. Stupid. Stupid. Stupid.

Mel thinks she could have done without show and tell Sunday she doesn't like either surprise she wants to get the fuck out of the basement she wants to think about something else. Maybe Cam was right maybe they were charmed. Past tense. Present tense Mel feels self-conscious she feels a little afraid.

In the garden out back they've planted everything
they can think of corn at one end squash acorn spaghetti
zucchini tomatoes peppers green red jalepeno cukes
beans string peas scallions carrots endive lettuce. Cam's
cantaloupe fill one corner of the plot. Gillian and Mel tend
the herbs mint basil fennel dill rosemary catnip they don't
have a cat. Bordering the edge of the garden where
thickets of trees separate them from the river they've
planted sunflowers already now four feet tall still growing.
A few things are starting to mature green tomatoes little
cukes. Nothing edible yet. Nobody asked the landlord if
they could dig up his yard or his secretary at Stamp
Enterprises Unlimited they just did. Bud thought they'd
need a rototiller he was in charge unofficially of the
garden the only one with any gardening know-how. But
with eight of them and shovels and hoes they found
borrowed even bought the earth got turned over well
enough better than that turned over chopped up mixed
loosened. They put bags and bags of manure in Matt
sprinkled in a couple bags of batshit he was crazy for the
idea who knows why. The plants they got across town at
a hothouse. They piled in Ron's minivan Gillian's Mazda
and drove over everybody made time nobody had more
pressing commitments. People other customers were
amused annoyed MattGillianBudAugustMattMelRoneven
Cam ran around picking up this that piling everything on
a cart shouting to each other do we want this or that or
could you find this or that. Planting they got dirty filthy
sweaty argued about setup layout what should go where
had pizzas for dinner beer wine even smoked some dope
forgot about themselves for an entire day and most of a
night had fun planted a garden. They agreed all of them
that it was more fun than they'd had since they were kids.
Work was like play. Things just happened turned out well.

Only Mel's taking a summer class. Everyone else is done for the year or studying for prelims or writing trying to write the diss. Gillian's teaching a summer class though and so is Matt second semester freshman composition. They've both taught it who knows how many times twice a semester most semesters for one two three four five six semesters not counting summers. It's lost its charm if it had any but it's only three days a week actual classroom time two hours a day. Bud and August are waiting tables catering in evenings on weekends. Ron's on fellowship he spends almost all day around The Mansion reading writing watching tv fighting with Mel over the reading chair in their room. Matt saved up money during the year he's around too though in his room mornings writing. Cam doesn't go out much no one really knows his deal. They spend some days putting finishing touches on The Mansion filling it with furniture. August is preternaturally skilled at finding curbed sofas coat racks bookcases chests of drawers tables lamps plants a filing cabinet things that are dented usually but not too damaged. She and Bud and Ron drive around and around the city cruising alleys in Ron's minivan picking stuff up dumpster-diving is what they call it though none of their finds are ever in the dumpsters but beside them. At times they're in direct competition with two men in a blue pickup it has no bumpers a SALVAGE sign painted on the rear gate the guys aren't filling a house they're making a living. One evening RonBudAugust beat the truck by minutes to a bedframe perfect condition if a little bulky and Ron makes a joke about how it was a close race maybe next time things will be different. The next morning Ron leaves The Mansion his tires all four are flat.

Gillian's not taking a summer class it's a good thing she needs a few months away from academia. Gillian hates graduate school mostly the people the graduate students uptight precise know-it-alls. She hates being corrected proved wrong in anything and graduate students do that. Correct her correct everyone when they get the chance. She hates it because she's a graduate student uptight precise if not a know-it-all then very careful about what she knows. So when she slips up makes a mistake is looked at funny pounced on corrected she grows furious. Mostly at herself. For slipping up. For giving the impression that she's not as smart as she wants to be thinks she is is terrified she isn't. But a single person can't contain the kind of fury she feels rage really the overflow of emotion she feels at herself when she makes mistakes is corrected is shown up proved wrong wrong wrong stupid. Dumb. Idiot. The people showing her up have to take some of the blame. And they do. Gillian hates graduate school mostly the people the graduate students uptight precise know-it-alls. Even if they're holding her to the higher standard that she wants to always achieve maintain surpass. Gillian hates herself for hating anyone. She's got an ethic inbuilt a reflex action that tells her it's wrong to hate to blame to be unkind cruel to judge. Who knows where it comes from. Matt's wondered. He knows she was raised a Christian sort of. Her grandmother was devout her mother a believer Gillian must have absorbed some of it the whole turn the other cheek rap is how Matt thinks of it. He knows too what tv she watched growing up this means a lot to him that she was only allowed to watch Disney as a child and Little House on the Prairie. Gillian's

mother was a devoted Michael Landon fan right up until
his death part of the loyal viewer base of Highway to
Heaven. He's never watched the show. Not Highway. Or
Little House. Never not once in all his life but he knows
about it the whole sweetness and light riff the show's
insistence on the need for a moral base the struggle of the
good Landonclan against the evils of the world the stern
father figure and the mother he's never heard much about.
He assumes she played the empathic foil to and the
hegemonic stooge of the stern Patriarch. What else could
she be. Later in life when she was older Gillian was
allowed to watch more tv. Her favorite characters were
Hawkeye Pierce Felix Unger Jim Rockford. In movies
Woody Allen. Matt knows because he's asked. They're all
good characters kind if neurotic moralizing liberals though
Rockford in a deflated hard knocks grumpy West Coast
kind of way. This is how Matt likes to understand her in
light of the tv she's liked still likes it seems to say something about her where she's coming from what she prefers
who she admires who she is. She's LandonAldaRandall
GarnerAllen or their alter egos. Moralizing kind hearted
neurotic self-critical intellectual. Even though she's got a
grudge against tv on the whole prefers to do things she
says in her spare time. Idle hands yada yada yada is what
Matt hears when she criticizes the tube. The thing is lately
Gillian hasn't much criticized tv. She doesn't much watch
it but she hasn't criticized it. She hasn't been much inclined. The way she hasn't been much inclined to criticize
anyone at least in The Mansion. Gillian doesn't hate
anyone there right now. She hasn't been tempted to she
doesn't yet trust everyone in The Mansion but there's no
hate against which she has to struggle nobody has acted
like graduate students around her at least not much. She
even feels like it might be okay if her guard slipped in
front of MattAugustBudRonMelCam and it goes without
saying Matt and she screwed up said or did something
stupid. They'd forgive or maybe even find a way to not

notice. When Matt leaves Matt and Mel in the tv room and comes to bed Gillian is naked waiting for him. Weird. Matt is the one who makes all the first moves. Gillian strips off his clothes she spreads her legs and pulls him in.

Matt feels good. It's summer it's warm. He's not taking classes he's teaching one. A summer session. Freshman composition. It's hard work the grading especially but he likes doing it. Mostly. So it's not exactly like work. Not when it goes well. And it's not all that time consuming a halftime job if that. He's got a lot of free time to himself. So he's been reading. And writing but not so much. He's been watching some tube. He's relaxed. He deserves it he worked hard last year a lot of teaching a lot of reading a lot of writing not a lot of break time. He feels good. Matt feels better than he has in past summers maybe better than ever before. It's The Mansion of course he knows it's The Mansion that's making the difference. This truth seems very straightforward to him and Matt prefers straightforward truths he likes knowing in a linear kind of way he knows he likes knowing this way. This worries him sometimes but most times he thinks that liking this kind of knowing doesn't mean he's stupid which it might. More that it means he doesn't have much imagination much capacity for invention difference. Fine he can't help this he's never had much capacity for imagination invention difference because he's never had much capacity for the kinds of things that would lead to them he's never had much capacity that is for doing for being with the world. Especially if that doing means being active engaging. He's not active. He's not engaging. In a way in

this way he's a living breathing case of entropy. Sort of.
He's energetic that is but in a way that always degrades
into a kind of inert flatness. Flat he's flat. Most of the time.
But not lethargic just single minded. What's usually on his
mind. Work work and resting up for waiting for work.
Who knows why. He's afraid of being distracted from his
tasks so only work. He's afraid of failure it's a miracle he
risked graduate school so work only work it's the only
thing that even vaguely promises success. He's boring a
dull boy why not work. He's shy work doesn't confound
him the way that people do so get to work. He's fixated
compulsive obsessive he can't let work go he can't mix it
with anything else it dilutes the purity. He's always been
convinced that he needs to be happy with what he's got.
And he's always got work if nothing else. So he works. A
lot all the time it's who he is. What a lot of crap. What a
perfectly single minded understanding of himself is what
Matt thinks. What a monocular load of bs. Which said
understanding being monocular illustrates just how single-
minded he is making the understanding of his single
mindedness right. Right. Not exactly. And anyway there's a
difference this summer he has The Mansion. It makes it's
been making the difference. Matt's not much given to
romantic visions of life The Mansion Has Changed His Life
etc. blah blah Turned Things Around For Him. It hasn't.
But when Matt gets up in the morning he works for a
while writes reads then he stops and has breakfast there's
someone to talk to almost always someone around besides himself and Gillian be it BudAugustRonMelMattor
Cam. Just a little chat a little company before he gets back
to work. It's nice it relaxes him it opens up his day to hear
someone else's voice ideas to share something anything in
the pause between the beats the blank space. He likes it
and at night he watches tv with Matt and now Mel's there
too at times and it's nice to have company. Watching isn't
anymore just a void his brain turned off but something
they can do together and actually talk about now and

then. He likes too to see how everyone in The Mansion lives it gives him ideas about his own life new ideas things he could have never come up with on his own he doesn't have much imagination. It all helps him relax. It's okay. Matt feels good.

August knows she shouldn't want a cat. So many reasons. She's not settled foremost she's moved twice in the past two years. And she'll move again sometime soon she's not sure when but it wouldn't be fair to the cat. Cats like to settle into one spot to know it a set turf to prowl. Besides when she moves when they move again she'll have to find a cat-friendly apartment building and they're not easy to come by. There's the cost too not a lot usually but what if the cat needs a vet that can add up. Besides there's everyone in The Mansion to consider maybe they don't like cats are allergic. August tells Bud that she sees the logic in all this but she doesn't care. She wants a cat she's going to get a cat.

I feel a need she tells Bud. I can't explain it but I feel like I have to have a cat right now. I need the connection.

Connection Bud asks.

To the world to an animal August says. She likes animals they ground her. She grew up with cats dogs birds fish. She feels they're conductors they help her complete a circuit between herself and something more elemental than human life. Something animal something else. She touches a dog a cat a horse a goat a chicken she feels a spark she's becoming animal. A little. I need to be loved by a cat she says. I need the kind of love only a cat can give. This is the short answer. August figures Bud should understand.

Bud nods he understands he guesses. August gives him the kind of love only an August can give it's not the same thing exactly but. He needs August love for too many reasons he can't bear the thought of not having it around. He kisses her. Whatever you want he says.

When she asks around everyone likes the idea even Matt who's allergic. He'll just run an air filter HEPA in his bedroom he'll be fine maybe it's time he saw about allergy shots anyway. No big deal. Maybe not a longhair though.

Mel's off schedule she's behind in reading for her seminar behind in pulling together a paper but it's summer why worry. Or why worry too much. If she can't stay up late nights hanging out with Matt and sometimes Matt watching the tube then what can she do. She likes Letterman she's not a fan exactly but he's entertaining if in a rut a little predictable nowadays. Conan O'Brien's better a little edgy absurd bizarre frenetic. She wants to push for cable in The Mansion that's where the best shows are MST3K Oz Dr. Katz it wouldn't cost much split eight ways. But really only she and Matt and sometimes Matt watch tv. So they'd have to split it three ways and then it's a cost. And who can afford that. Not her. And anyway she shouldn't want that much tv. Correction. She shouldn't watch that much tv wanting is okay. Correction. Wanting is not so okay and she knows it. Don't want too much too often in life love attention recognition security excitement success acceptance. Don't want these things from parents don't want them from friends lovers professors yourself. No one not even everyone all taken together can give you these things or at least as much of them as you want. Or in

her case past tense. Wanted. She's got a handle on needing.
She doesn't need as much doesn't want as much. Or if she
does she doesn't let herself notice she doesn't give in to
needing. She's got enough. She's happy. Which is what
anyone who knows Mel would say it's what everyone in
The Mansion thinks about her. Mel has got it together. Mel
is always up cheerful focussed full of concentration good
energy conversation friendliness. Mel's got it together. Mel's
good to be around. Mel's smart organized hip she's Mel.

      She's horny she's been horny all summer it's the heat
it's the humidity it's gotta be. It's not. She's lived through
summers like this before moist tropical ones and they
didn't make her horny. They made her tired. They gave
her prickly heat a rash yeast infections. So it's not the heat
it's not the humidity. It's just this summer. It's The Mansion
something about it it's making her horny itchy and it's not
that her mind's sleepy groggy not that her body's taking
over the slow throbbing of blood in her stiff clit putting
her cranky mind asleep. Her mind's sharp she's alert she
feels awake energized excited. And. Horny. On top of it.
She feels like part of an open circuit flowing energy. She's
feeding off it buzzed a little feverish getting a lot of work
done staying up till all hours watching tv talking and then
up again the next morning. But she needs to shut down
now and then complete the circuit take a break from it all.
Once in a while. Once a day usually. Whether Ron's
awake or not when she gets into bed if he's not awake he
soon is. She strips him down strips herself down puts her
lips around his cock takes his balls in one hand opens
herself with the other.

Ron's hard when he wakes up he's hard when he eats lunch hard drinking beer in the evening hard when he falls asleep. Not literally hard not always. Sometimes he's metaphorically hard he's got a virtual boner virtual meaning his hard on is waiting for the tiniest impulse to become actual. He thinks it's the heat it's hot and moist this summer it's like living inside genitalia a woman's organ he thinks he's surrounded by pussy. Is how he likes to think. Not that he'd tell anyone this it's absurd. This is how turned on he is this summer he's thinking ridiculous thoughts. Living inside a woman's pussy. Gross. But kinda cool Ron thinks. Last night like most nights when he woke up in the halfdark he felt Mel's lips around his cock when he looked up her legs rose on either side of his head coming together at her bush her back was arched just a little bit her hand was spreading her lips he raised his head he pulled her down. It's like this every night. To begin with. And then things get crazy he and Mel are fucking like rabbits like dogs like. Ron wonders what elephants fuck like giraffes camels geese pigs why no one ever fucks like them. It doesn't seem fair they probably fuck with as much excitement and devotion as anyone. As anyone in The Mansion everyone's getting a lot this summer. As far as Ron can tell. It's not just him and Mel it's Matt and Gillian Bud and August. The Mansion's not a new building it's solid but it's not all that soundproof and the couples are in rooms pretty much next to each other all on the second floor you can hear the fucking through the walls. When he comes Bud sounds like he's just heard a bad joke a pun he groans ohhhh. In a deep voice. And

August whimpers she sounds like she's crying almost it's
very high pitched ooooaaahh. Gillian talks during sex a
constant low monotone it sounds dirty wicked naughty is
what Ron thinks. He never hears Matt Matt never makes
noise one. Ron wonders if downstairs Matt can hear all of
them through the ceiling. He wonders if upstairs Cam can
hear them through the floor. If they can Ron thinks it must
drive them nuts out of their frickin minds. Christ.

What's worst for Bud is knowing that if he can hear
Mel and Ron and Gillian and Matt. Screwing. Whatever it
is they do that makes them make the sounds they make
thumping squeaking flopping moaning groaning growling
whining. If he can hear them they can hear him. And
August. Of course. This is tough for Bud because he can't
let on that it bothers him. That they hear him. It's not like
him to be bothered being bothered is not who he is who
he wants to be. It's not progressive left he's a hippie an
intellectual hippie but a hippie nonetheless in resale
clothes Salvation Army Goodwill and Birkenstocks. Bud
wears hooded pullover jackets made in South America has
hemp blankets on the bed pins on his backpack that say
MEAT IS MURDER SAVE THE PLANET MEAN PEOPLE
SUCK. He's a walking cliché but he thinks clichés have
meaning too and sometimes cliches are the best ways of
getting at meanings. And his are idealistic. So there. But
according to his rules he's supposed to be open to sharing
a little privacy hints of what people do behind closed
doors. He's supposed to be open to receptive to communal lifestyles tearing down boundaries new environments
come-what-may. He's supposed to be open to exposing

himself. He's not supposed to be embarrassed not supposed to be prudish not supposed to let himself be governed by the morals of not his parents hippies themselves
but of his grandparents repressed fifties squares. Squares
it's what they were they knew the rules didn't break the
rules. He's not supposed to want rules not supposed to
want anything that's defined or crystallized. What's crystallized is static and what's static is dead. But Bud cringes
when in bed August moans when they bang up against
the wall when one edge of their futon frame lifts off the
floor and comes cracking back down. He's taken to
playing music when they have sex Van Morrison or The
Grateful Dead. Blues Traveler. He can't play it loud
enough though to cover everything it would be rude. He
doesn't worry all the time he forgets to be bothered a lot
of the time he's never distracted when he comes. But
always right after. Always when August comes she's got a
high pitched moan. He's troubled when someone else in
The Mansion has sex while he and August have sex. It's
perverse but it makes him feel like they're all having sex
together and this gets under his skin. It's wrong. He can't
tell August how he feels.

Sometimes at night Matt can hear at the same time
six people having sex. Some are louder than others at
least for him Bud and August are above his room. But he
can hear all the others too Matt and Gillian Ron and Mel.
Sometimes. It's not always that everyone's doing it at the
same time but when that happens Matt wants to crawl
under his bed stuff cotton in his ears walk out the front
door and sit on the porch. It makes him feel lonely

disconnected simultaneously immersed in The Mansion
but outside it as well the single guy downstairs on the
fringe of things not a part of a larger animal connection
between the other bodies. Oh well it might be tough for
him but it adds spice to the book he'll suffer for his art.
He'll suffer in his art. Whatever. Even Cam's been sneaking a woman in only Matt knows about it. Being the single
guy he has time on his hands he notices things. And he's
seen her on the livecam now and then he tunes in from
his room. Why Cam is sneaking her in not bringing her in
the front door he doesn't know but he knows he's sneaking her in. Cam. And getting some love obviously some
heat friction some human some animal connection. Matt's
downstairs with his fist. His computer. He's not a porn
junky not exactly but he goes online more and more now
looking for filthy pictures the filthiest pictures he can find
spread legs spread lips gaping anuses with fists in them
blowjobs bondage simulated rapes fucking sucking foot-
fetishes piercings waifs animals orgies tag-team intercourse
in live-time feed complete with sound bleached-blondes
with red painted lips semen stretching from their squinting
eyes to their mouths women peeing shitting ingesting both
leather whips fishhooks breasts the size of his head
swollen cocks crammed between them jism oozing. It
keeps his mind from running loose the way it does when
he feels too lonely he wonders what's wrong with him
why he's not with someone what he's missing where
people are what they're doing what they must think of
him. It helps relieve the pressure too gives him something
to beat off to and he does that a lot lately his cock is
chafed even. Boom boom boom groan moan whine starts
upstairs and he gets online. Blows a little steam. Then
usually he blows a little dope including some of the buds
he's plucked off the plants in the basement.

It's not Cam's idea to keep Karen a secret it's Karen's.
She doesn't know anyone in The Mansion well she knows
them all but she doesn't know them well. She sees them
MattGillianBudAugustMelRon around the department but
she doesn't talk to them. They're all younger meaning
she's older. Not physically more that she's been around a
whole lot longer. Around the department working on her
degree she came in with a whole different cohort the
group of people she got to know when she had the time
the energy the will. Now she's almost finished and she
doesn't have much time for anything but getting finished
getting her dissertation done defending. Moving on. If she
talks to anyone anymore it's through email responding to
calls for papers writing reviews for journals setting up
conference dates trying to arrange publications looking for
a faculty position. She writes to people all around the
country people she knows personally people she knows
via email people who are a part of an extended community shaped by academic interests. It makes her feel
spread thin sometimes belonging to this community
communicating via email letters phone calls mostly. But it
makes her feel good too like she's widening her circles
spreading out becoming a part of something big bigger.
Than U of F than graduate student life. She's cultivating it
carefully this community she knows it will be hers for life
her peers her audience the people she'll turn to for intellectual stimulation. She won't turn to the people that will
someday soon be around her on a more constant basis all
sorts of types with all sorts of interests and none of those
the same as hers. It's what happens when you fill out a
teaching position at a small college somewhere. She'll
spend the rest of her adult life surrounded by a bunch of
misogynist backwater fucks is what she thinks and the

students will always already be eighteen years old with
their eighteen-year-old attitudes and small town locals
shopping at Walmart and smoking generic brand cigarettes
and hitting their kids but stops herself you can't afford to
think this way. She takes Cam's foot lays it on the small
round of her stomach. She just doesn't have the energy to
get to know anyone in The Mansion. She'd almost like to
but it would take too much and she's not interested in
small talk she's got no stomach for that. So she comes to
see Cam late at night. She comes in the back door he
leaves it open up the back stairs into Cam's attic. She digs
the attic it feels like a garrett she digs Cam he's quiet and
a little maniacal looking intense. She digs bossing Cam
around at least sexually. Which he seems to get off on she
tells him what to do and when to do it and how to do it.
Sometimes she makes him eat her for twenty thirty minutes she can't imagine his lips tongue jaw don't get stiff
sore numb but he doesn't complain. She digs his computer setup the livecam. Tonight she wore her mask the
one Cam bought it covers her forehead eyes and nose just
below the nose it has long whiskers stretching out like a
cat's. That's all just the mask nothing else she let the cam
run while she posed danced bent over her legs spread in
front of almost touching the livecam. Online she calls
herself Pussy Queen of the Pirates.

Besides Cam only Mel and Ron have people over and
then not for long to watch a baseball game on the tube. A
beer or two. Then they all go out for a drink at a local bar
maybe to hear a band. Nobody's felt much need for guests
there's plenty of company around The Mansion. Or at least

this is how Matt looks at it he's got all the company he
needs period. Matt feels the same way he's been neglecting
his nonMansion friends he knows he should knock it off.
But The Mansion's the thing now everything seems to
depend on it. There's a lot at stake here. So. Focus. August
doesn't feel settled yet like she knows the contours of The
Mansion well enough to wear it like a coat a shirt a pair of
socks to be able to entertain in it and be relaxed. Bud will
be ready for company when August is whatever whenever
he tends to follow her cues. She seems to be more in tune
with these things. Mostly. Gillian doesn't much like having
people in her home anyway she never has. If she wants to
enjoy the company of her friends she meets them for coffee
lunch a movie shopping whatever but she doesn't like to
invite them into her home.

Guests involve managed boundaries she says.

They do Matt asks.

Sure they do she says why do you think people clean
like lunatics before people come over. So they can rein-
force boundaries.

Like Matt says.

Like what's public and what's private and what
people can see and what they can't she says. Guests
involve creating an ideal of your home inside your home.

They do Matt asks.

Which is just enough to piss Gillian off. A little.
Because she knows Matt is being a pain in the ass he
enjoys being a pain in the ass making other people talk
and talk and talk and maybe they're not ready to talk. Not
fully ready.

No really Matt says like how.

Like all unmentionables get put away Gillian says
and the good towels come out. And that's just the start
who wants to be bothered with worrying about things like
that. For someone else's sake.

And BudandAugustandMattandMelandRonandCam
are different.

Mostly Gillian says. My mess is their mess. In a way. The dynamics are different.

With me too Matt says laughs. He pretends he forgot to include himself with BudandAugustandMattandMeland RonandCam. He didn't forget he doesn't think he's in the same boat with them where public and private are concerned they're not finks and he is. Around him Gillian can never quite have the privacy she wants or imagines she has. She's a character in his book. After all. Her life's an open text. How do you tell someone that.

When someone does come to The Mansion for a visit it's August's friend Anny. August's still not quite ready for guests when she invites Anny over and Anny's husband too but she's got to take the plunge she's got to start entertaining she's nothing if not a social animal. She misses company dinner guests sitting around in the evening drinking wine beer talking burning candles listening to music. Which they do in The Mansion already at times everyone who lives there but not in an organized way. August likes an event a get-together she likes planning things out organizing setting a nice table. And whatever's missing in terms of feeling comfortable hosting in The Mansion will be made up for by the comfort her friends will bring. In. To The Mansion. Guests do that for her friends help situate her maybe that's all she needs in fact to make her feel finally fully at home in The Mansion. Friends over to help her finish finding The Mansion as a place a space a home. Though at first the logistics are weird. Who will be where when. August needs the kitchen she needs the dining room she needs the living room or maybe the porch after supper. She needs all the things that a hostess needs when hostessing. But there are six other people in The Mansion they need those things too not counting Bud and how do you work around that. Not a problem Matt says he's going to hang out in his room he's got work to do and Gillian and Matt have been meaning to go out for dinner for a while. Ron and Mel are heading down to The Pelican to watch the game and no one's seen Cam all day he might not even be upstairs at all.

The problem is that Anny's not a normal guest that is a normal person. She's uncontrollable the worst kind of theater type is how Bud thinks of her. She was in too many awful plays in high school in college a theater major not too smart but enthusiastic to the point of being hyper always dramatic emotive. Always wanting everyone to catch her mood to get that group buzz to join in the fun. Even when there's not a mood a group buzz just her mood her buzz. She's a mood bully Bud thinks always cramming her need for drama down everyone's throats never listening to anything anyone says never cares what they want. It drives Bud nuts he doesn't like joining in on her kind of fun in any circumstance he's a little more laid back than that. He finds that life needs pauses reflection if one is going to gather one's thoughts if one's going to concentrate. And he likes sharp comments witty points smart conversation not unreflective enthusiasm. So when Anny comes over her husband in tow the guy's not a talker a smiler mostly a shoulder shrugger he follows Anny around like a lost puppy Bud's stomach sinks. He's glad really glad that GillianMattRonMelandCam aren't around and not just because they aren't there to witness Anny's grand tour of The Mansion including a quick peek into everyone's rooms they won't mind will they. Hey Matt nice to meet you. Not just that but they're not there to hear again and again Anny say that The Mansion is the coolest thing on the planet no really what an awesome house. Yes those things especially at first. But then as the evening goes on he's glad that they're not home their absence clarifies things for him. How he feels about the people around him. What's what and who's who in other words he begins to understand at least one division between the spheres of his life. Anny and her husband are friends but they're guests they'll go home they're not a substantial part of his life. GillianMattMattRonMelandCam are friends but they're not guests they'll be coming home they'll be home when they're in The Mansion. That means that they're different sorts of friends. Which means something. Anny declares at the end of the evening she's had a little too much wine that she loves The Mansion it's the greatest place she wants to meet everyone who lives here she wants to spend all her time here she wishes she lived in The Mansion. Her husband just smiles nods. It means he likes it too The Mansion Bud supposes. August is excited it went well she thinks she's lifted by Anny's voluble friendship sweeping gestures positive exclamations. She sure needs a lot of clear encouragement sometimes Bud thinks unequivocal gushing affirmations of herself her surroundings her life. August.

Matt's not working on his dissertation the one he's supposed to be working on. The one his advisor his

committee expects to see at first in pieces and then as a
whole if not an opus a solid book of research eventually
publishable. But he says to Matt it doesn't mean he's not
working. He's writing the story of his life. Which includes
his friends. By just being in other words he's becoming a
writer he's getting some work done. One must he says
speak *with* write *with* the world with a part of the world
with people to be a writer to write. And really you don't
even really need to talk at all but just create a conspiracy a
collision of love and hatred assemble be in the middle on
the line of encounter between an internal world and the
external world. Be in the middle. It's being in the middle
that leads to writing it's being in the middle that's always
an assemblage one that produces utterances that don't
have as their cause a subject that would act as a subject of
enunciation any more than they are related to subjects as
subjects of utterance. You see what I mean. If things work
correctly the utterance is the product of an assemblage
that is always collective it brings into play within us and
outside us populations multiplicities territories becomings
effects events. What he means he says is that proper
names don't designate subjects but things that happen at
least between two terms that are not subjects but agents
elements. Proper names are not the names of persons but
of peoples and tribes flora and fauna military operations
or typhoons collectives limited companies and production
studios. Which he says as a point is a little off the track of
his argument. What he means to be saying at least right
now is that the author is a subject of enunciation. But the
writer. Who is not an author. Is not an author he emphasizes. He's himself a writer he's writing. Not authoring.
The writer invents assemblages starting from assemblages
that invented him he makes one multiplicity pass into
another. The difficult part is making all the elements of a
nonhomogenous set converge making them function
together. Structures are linked to conditions of homogene-
ity but assemblages are not. Matt's quite sure he has no

idea what the fuck Matt is talking about he nods smiles raises an eyebrow. Matt gets the picture Matt's not quite hearing what he's saying he's hearing it but not following. So he says life isn't up on the stage. It's out there in the audience. First I wanted to study what others have had to say about it. Sukenick. Now I want to write about it by living it. After that who knows. He certainly doesn't. Does any of this in the end have anything to do with Sukenick. Check for yourself Matt says. What Matt says. Check what.

Ron gets mugged on his way home from West Bank Café he'd had a Vietnamese dish been with three friends not GillianMattMatt AugustBudCam or even Mel. He'd been with Andy and Angela and Ellen. A normal evening a few drinks some fish in a clay pot lemongrass stew shrimp fried rice. Ron paid with his credit card got from everyone else their tabs in cash put it in his pocket an interest-free advance on his card. Sort of. Not that that was the plan just the way it happened and Ron needed the cash. Then Ron he's telling not Mel who's not home but GillianMattMattAugustBudCam in the living room his hands are shaking he decided to walk back to The Mansion it's only a mile or so the weather was nice. Angela didn't think it was a good idea but he insisted set off walking he had the money in his front pocket it was a big wad. He hadn't even tried to stuff it in his wallet. He's not hurt not hurt the guy didn't even touch him really he had just appeared out of nowhere in a sweatshirt the hood pulled over his head and sunglasses had motioned with his hand in his pocket said give me your wallet. Which Ron did it had a five and two ones which Ron says just pissed the guy off he came closer to him and said empty all your pockets. Which Ron did he wasn't even that scared not yet just surprised startled upset that he might lose all his spending money that big wad of cash. Then it got freaky Ron says I didn't get a good look at the guy's face but when I pulled out that wad of cash he came up within inches of me I could smell his breath it smelled like meat. It smelled like hamburger not McDonald's hamburger or cookout hamburger just like meat. Not spoiled meat. Just meat. He looked at the wad of cash he poked me in the stomach he said I think you better come with me. And Ron says I started shaking. I had a coppery feeling in my mouth I felt like my skin was dripping I was sweating so hard I was so scared. And he just left. He took the seven dollars out of my wallet dropped the five and two ones on the ground and then took my wad of money he took my wallet and walked off he didn't take my seven dollars Ron says he holds them out they're right there in front of them. He took my wallet. Then I walked home Ron says I just kept going in the same direction I'd been going before and now I'm here he says.

Bud says that Ron should call the police. Even if he wasn't hurt. Even if it's been a few days. He says the police need to know there's a mugger out there in a hood in the neighborhood holding people up. Ron's not sure he's busy he'd rather forget it the cops know there are muggers out there. So what else is new. Matt's with Ron he's pretty sure that calling the police would be an exercise in futility he's a got a general notion that most actions most people ever take are pretty much only that. Exercises in futility. But people do what they think they ought to they're obeying some cultural imperative some abstract sense of what's right they follow the rules on the off chance that they're really the right things. To follow. But it's really Matt says just one more version of covering your ass Matt spent ten years working in the real world that's what it's called at least the real world. Before graduate school. You toe the line in every instance you fill out the appropriate forms in the appropriate ways you never make a move without consulting informing someone else. You do nothing without permission you always make sure every problem all the problems that always happen no matter what anyone does can be traced to someone else's door. Not yours. See Why A Matt says cover your ass. Matt's never going to recover he doesn't think from his job it's not just this this dim view of the value of calling on public servants. It's that everything is like this he's got a dim view of the world. He doesn't want to but he can't help see everything around him in businesslike terms tits for tats backs being scratched even friendships as the exchange of goods as long as there are goods to be exchanged. Words of support for something in return who knows what someone to sit next to at the movies. Relationships just more of this but more complicated he thinks most women know it all too well he wonders if they think about it. Much. He doesn't let any of it bother him not much he's not a teenager angst ridden over the ways of the world. He plays along it's how things are he doesn't kid himself about what's what. He secretly wants to not think this way wishes he could believe trust like love just because. He thinks Bud does maybe and August and Mel and it makes him nervous. They either know something he doesn't or they're better people capable of seeing more being more. Or they're in for a vicious fall. Which he doesn't think would stop them from being who they are. He doesn't think. Which puzzles him. What Matt really wants is to avoid having cops around The Mansion. He supposes it wouldn't hurt for Ron to stop into the stationhouse for a few minutes. To make a report.

Terry stops by wanders over to the porch one evening they're most of them sitting around. He doesn't say anything at first nods. It's a cool evening after a hot day a breeze coming in off the lake. Cooled off nice he says. His shop the shop he works in doesn't have ac at least not in the bays it was a bitch today. In this heat. They have ac in the front office he says and the parts department. And the waiting room. He laughs when he does he doesn't sound healthy it's like he's got cotton candy in his lungs. Then he coughs. Customers wouldn't be too happy if the waiting room was as hot as the shop he says sounds like he wouldn't be unhappy if the customers weren't happy. Ron offers him a beer asks about everyone else heads into the kitchen and comes back with an armful of bottles. Terry studies the label says Porter huh never had Sierra Nevada doesn't sound like he wants it now. Takes a sip. Shrugs meaning his opinion is beer is beer but if people want to piss their money away.

Looks like you're settling in pretty good he says.

Nobody says anything what's there to say. Matt nods.

Even planted a garden he says not exactly a statement but not a question either. From his shirt pocket under where it says Terry he pulls out a pack of Camels.

August sits up straight she's on the porch steps she asks do you garden.

Another laugh more cotton candy Terry looks at August. Nope. Not tomatoes anyway. He grins when he does it's not a happy grin it says instead he's getting away with something it's a smirk. From the pack of camels he pulls out a joint lights it offers it around. Everyone declines he shrugs Matt thinks about accepting just to be neighborly. Instead he says no thanks. Terry nods. August excuses herself goes into The Mansion.

August knows Terry's type. She's spent enough of her life being welcome to others being friendly openminded interested that she's met all kinds it's all about meeting different people hearing different points of view isn't it. Yes but. She's run across many types and she hasn't liked them all and she knows Terry's. Type. She thinks she does. And she doesn't like the type. Not that she's completely sure about him she's not making any final judgments. But she's got suspicions. He's not mean but not nice friendly but in a self-interested way not pushy but intrusive. Understands boundaries respects them if it's a matter of law but mostly pushes. Them. Others'. Who knows why maybe for the pure pleasure maybe that's okay. Maybe not. Ends up brutalizing the weak. The kind. The friendly open-minded interested. August. Who's known his type all her life. Her parents knew the type even associated with it now and then on occasion at parties they hung around with all sorts. At least when August was young. Everyone was on the same side of something at the time part of the same movement if they were of one generation they were one. Was the idea. Was something they taught August in the abstract made her in her own day lean toward causes environmentalism vegetarianism antinuke action all group efforts. All group efforts mean being part of a group accepting everyone dealing with everyone August knows. She thinks she shouldn't judge Terry. Still she doesn't want to be anywhere near him she's afraid she's in the wrong it bothers her she knows better. She feels the same way anymore about her parents not that they're bad types. That she doesn't want to be anywhere near them she suspects she's in the wrong it bothers her she knows better. She sees her parents at least five or six times a year.

Matt's been watching tv all evening. After a time he wonders where Ron and Mel are whether they've gone to bed. On the way to the bathroom he stops outside their door it's cracked open. He looks without looking sees Mel naked on her back her legs spread knees up feet flat on the mattress Ron's head at her crotch. Ron's naked too leaning back on his legs but leaning forward also on his elbows fetal looking his ass facing the door. He's so skinny his arms wrapped around the outside of Mel's legs his hands reaching up touching her stomach her breasts. Her breasts. They're larger than Matt thought they're spilling over the side of her rib cage. Mel's head is twisted back on a pillow her mouth open her eyes aren't. Ron's ass. His head bobs up around around down. Then Mel's eyes are open for a second she stiffens raises a hand she sees Matt in the crack at the door. She doesn't know it's Matt. Then she knows it's Matt her hand moves toward Ron's head she starts to sit up. Ron thinks she's coming his hands move up he starts to pinch her nipples she doesn't say anything he pinches harder. Matt steps away. He can still see in but he's backing away his heart beating he can hear it in his ears. Mel's eyes close her head drops back on the pillow she moans squeezes Ron's head between her thighs. She is coming. He thinks. Matt could've used the downstairs bathroom it was empty.

It bugs Cam that the livecam goes unused he went to some effort to set it up. He thought it would be interesting fun exciting he thought it would make people happy. It doesn't the livecam doesn't seem to make anyone in The Mansion any of these things. What it makes them is uncomfortable. This is what Cam uncovers. Mel for one when Cam asks her about the livecam she says there's no way he's going to get her on that thing. Just keep it away she says keep it out of my life. I've got enough problems she doesn't mean problems she means things. She says I've got enough things to deal with. Ron's with Mel. Sort of. That is he doesn't mind the idea of posing for a photo now and then maybe or maybe not but he's not about to write anything online not his autobiography or anything else. He's not a fiction writer so fiction's out too. Why would he write that anyway. And for whom Ron doesn't see the point. Cam doesn't say anything why bother. If Ron doesn't want to then. But Bud doesn't want to either he hates the idea of virtual reality he's got a real world to live in he says before stopping and saying not that there's anything wrong with having a livecam. I mean if that's your thing. August is okay with goofing around upstairs but nothing serious the aquarium idea is growing on her or some variation on it it might be fun but she doesn't think she has the time to spend. Gillian doesn't have time to spare either she says to play around. Matt says the same thing maybe he says to Gillian we can play around with it

together sometime just a few pictures a little doodling.
Gillian looks at him Cam looks at Gillian. Just keep it
away from me is what Mel says. She bites off the end of
her sentence. Cam wonders how that sentence should
have could have might have ended. He wonders if Mel
thinks he's a pathetic computer obsessed dork alone in his
garret just him and his screen and his online friends
unable to have normal human relations. Is this what they
all think of him. What about Matt.

Matt's crazy for the idea of the livecam he just hasn't
gotten around to using it. When Cam approaches him this
is what he says. He likes how the livecam is a tool not just
for flashing pictures but for telling a story their story the
story of The Mansion. Matt thinks the livecam offers
unique ways of telling stories in fragments in bursts he
likes that it will reach out in unpredictable ways to nontra-
ditional audiences. Pretty cutting edge stuff Matt says to
Cam he's making fun of the livecam of himself he doesn't
want to seem over excited. But Matt really does dig the
livecam and being excited is good it's what he needs right
now is something exciting something that will keep him
writing. He's burned out on his novel it doesn't seem to
be moving anywhere. He thinks it needs a jump start.
    If you're going to write about The Mansion Cam says.
    I know Matt says he'll have to be low-key. He knows
what people think of the livecam. He can't expect much
cooperation nobody else wants to play. Well. Maybe
they'll change their minds when they see what he does.
Maybe they'll end up wanting to write a little or at least
contribute themselves visually. Maybe not. Maybe they'll

get pissed off maybe he'll be looking for trouble forcing
the livecam on them he'll see how it goes maybe he won't
include them. Maybe he won't tell them what he's up to.
What they don't know won't hurt them. Right. He won't
use their real names so where's the harm. He can get a
digital camera he can take their pictures anywhere any-
time without their knowing. Scratch that he'll sneak
pictures of them only when they're in public places in The
Mansion and out. He's not a voyeur after all is he.

When Matt goes upstairs to use the livecam Cam's
not around. The computer's on Cam always leaves it on
when Matt moves the mouse kills the screensaver there's
no text. There's a picture on the screen it's one that's been
saved it's CamBudGillianAugustMattRonMattMel against a
backdrop of white there are chairs in front of beside them
a ratty brown loveseat in the back and so on. There's a
window. Matt turns on the QuickCam after a minute Matt's
standing there thinking the screen changes now it shows
him. In the room. Thinking. He sits down. He writes

The Children of Frankenstein

The cows. Paul loves to watch the cows in the meadows north of the city he drives there when he's upset. What always strikes him is the way their rears end in rectangles. Rectangled and a little raised like the sterns of old galleons. Their teats bulge like rubber gloves their noses are pink and each has its own geography of black and white. The cows watch him with their dumb eyes and he likes them because they're dumb. He likes the cows because they're big. He likes the cows because they eat their grass and they're content. He likes the cows because they flick flies away with their tails. He likes the cows because their voices are full and mellow. He likes the cows because of their heavy slow step. He likes the cows because they run in slow motion. He likes the cows because they sniff the wind. He likes the cows because their drool is beautiful in the sun. He likes the cows because they're at peace. The cows. The cows. The cows.

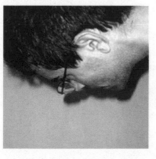

Mel wants to know who Paul is he sure looks a lot like you she says. Ha. Matt says he doesn't know exactly who Paul is. He's Paul he supposes though he never drives north of the city he never watches cows. But he thinks he might like watching the cows he likes the prospect cows are peaceful rhythmic real.

If real means really smelly Mel says have you ever been close to a cow.

Yes Matt thinks at the state fair he always thought they smelled warm and healthy. No not really he says you have.

My mother's brother she says has a farm had a farm. He raised cows for slaughter. She looks into the monitor they're in the attic she sees herself. My cousins when they were teenagers used to fuck them. I watched one time I was about ten. They had to stand on stools to reach you know to get it in. It made her sick. To see them groping around humping animals like animals it was carnal violent brutish.

Matt can ask politely he can plead he can say whatever he wants but Mel doesn't want to appear on the livecam she simply doesn't want to. She blushes she doesn't want to share her life with strangers. She doesn't want to write about life in The Mansion she wouldn't know what to say. Or what would be safe to say.

How about what you just told me Matt asks. Mel looks sick at the thought. How about I write it Matt asks. How about we never show more than part of your face on screen Matt asks. How about if I call you Joan. How about it. If there's anyone in The Mansion that Matt wants to say yes to him yes about the livecam it's Mel.

THE CHILDREN OF FRANKENSTEIN

So Joan won't help him make a homepage even the idea makes her flinch. Paul doesn't press after a point he can read body language hers is saying no. She seems repulsed. By him his idea the homepage. Fine. Whatever. Paul doesn't need her participation he doesn't need anyone's in fact not Joan's not Cloud's not Evelyn's not Wind's not Feather's not Ralph's not Al's. The Children's page will be his own project it'll take up where his novel leaves off it'll have pictures. And an audience Paul thinks. An immediate audience maybe. If anyone's interested in reading the pages he'll wait and see maybe they'll click in for the photos the visual record of their lives. Paul's already ordered his digital camera it's a sweet one shooting at over two megapixels per picture it was pricey but worth it.

THE CHILDREN OF FRANKENSTEIN

Joan hasn't been able to sleep for a week. She's stopped even trying to sleep she stays in the tv room until three or four in the morning not watching tv but sitting staring thinking. The summer's ending she's got a seminar paper due in a week and she's stymied. Not a clue about her topic or rather too many ideas she can't settle on one but it's not that. It's the end of the summer. Or what the powers that be say is the end of the summer the end of the summer term two weeks until fall term two more classes to take two to teach. Joan's not naive if anything she's the opposite of naive she's got a darkly realistic view of things and she knows that life in The Mansion has been good so far because it's been summer sunny expansive

new fresh food from the garden tomatoes beans cukes the flat smell of eucalyptus of juniper like a good dream when the wind stirs the sunstilled woods or the heavy wine of some flower maybe honeysuckle. Now it's almost not summer and a new rhythm will start and Joan doesn't know what kind of music it will make. She expects the worst nothing specific not yet but the worst. Regular semesters are always a struggle for survival you get one long breath at the beginning of the term and then four months underwater. How can people get along in close quarters if they can't breathe. Maybe she's worrying too much why doesn't she sit down and write. Cloud can't sleep he doesn't mind sleeping alone but he hasn't gotten laid in a week. After this summer of sex it feels like an eternity his balls are swollen horny. Dissatisfied.

The Children of Frankenstein

Paul can't sleep. He smokes too much. Again. For a while he didn't. Smoke. But he's started again why not he's got an air filter in his room be bought it because of Feather's cat but it catches smoke too. So he smokes a pack a day maybe a little less a little more. It jacks him up. It relaxes him up. It relaxes him too but he knows that he wouldn't need to be slowed down if it didn't jack him up in the first place nicotine drives his metabolism into a frenzy. He has to drink coffee when he smokes the two go together. So he's jittery he smokes more to cut the edge and so it goes. He can't sleep more than four or five hours a night. He can imagine the end of his life dying of cancer emphysema in agonizing pain plugged into breathing tubes one day he'll drag himself to his hospital window he'll drag himself through it had better be on an upper floor. His final line of flight. Plagiarizing up to his last breath though he supposes at that point no one will catch his reference so what. It will please him or he thinks it will. One final allusion repetition recreation. A tribute to poor Gilles. No one else in The Mansion smokes no one else he knows smokes. Only five years before everyone smoked. Now people have quit it's the right thing to do healthwise. Paul can't stand it when people add the word wise to the ends of other words but it's what people do. Along with not smoking which is passé uncool unhealthy a financial drain. At least for good kids of the middle class like their parents before them they smoked then quit at some appointed time after college after getting a job getting pregnant whatever. They were naughty naughty naughty then not. Paul's sure that the not naughty attitude pleases the insurance companies they're probably responsible for defining naughty and not but he's got other things to think about. For instance Joan she's been up all night lately too she's taken to going outside at the weirdest hours two three in the morning and sitting on the lawn caught in the moonlight cross-legged on the green grass. They don't keep things mowed anymore. She stares at the garden not The Mansion. Paul doesn't think that sitting outside alone at night is all that good an idea not in their neighborhood. He keeps an eye on her without her knowing he watches her and watches her out the kitchen window until she comes in again. By then he's back in his room. Paul's full of energy nowadays but he looks like hell. He's lost weight his hair is too long he's got circles under his eyes.

THE CHILDREN OF FRANKENSTEIN

Wind's taken up catering he needs the cash. Ralph and Feather let him tag along when their boss needs an extra hand. They've been catering for a while all sorts of gigs bar mitzvahs birthdays weddings setting tables setting plates clearing plates washing dishes. Wind knows in a way he's being stupid. He's got no time for extra work but he can't help himself. He's panicked he's worried about money he's worried about school about doing well about teaching standing in front of rooms full of people. He's worried about Evelyn because she's worried too. Probably about the same things he's worried about though he's never sure with her he just knows that when

she worries she hums not through her mouth but through her skin. She exudes an aura of anxiety in pulses waves. The way he looks at it is Evelyn has a dark side as well as a bright. Like the moon. The dark side you never see that's why it's dark you just know it's there from things that pop out. Like when someone is afraid of let's say brussels sprouts Evelyn acts like the rug is going to be yanked out from under her and she'll be left spinning in midspace like the moon. Alone. When Evelyn was a kid her parents got divorced. She went to live with her mother. Then when her father remarried she went to live with her father and stepmother. Then when her father got divorced again she went to live with her mother and stepfather. When her mother and stepfather split she was old enough to go to college. Which didn't make any difference Evelyn was already blasted into orbit. Her parents chipped in for the shrink but after three years she dropped psychoanalysis not because it did no good but because she didn't want to spend the rest of her life preparing for the rest of her life. Wind thinks that Evelyn loves him. One reason Evelyn loves him is because he worries. When he worries he panics when he panics he does everything he can to make the world less worrisome for him for Evelyn. If he's worried about school he studies all night. If he's worried about teaching he overprepares. If he's worried about money about cost of living about using up his nest egg he does what he has to do. He caters. He hates catering. He helps make Evelyn feel safe. He's a rock. He even looks like a rock dark and short and solid all muscle no fat an inscrutable look on his face his skin mottled and pitted with acne scars.

THE CHILDREN OF FRANKENSTEIN

Sometimes when Paul thinks about people he thinks about them in terms of geology. He thinks that we all have faults in our personalities but usually they lie below the surface layers in the deep substructure until some shift in the crust brings them out and we're shaken up. Paul thinks that this kind of fissure is opening up in the people around him in Joan for one.

THE CHILDREN OF FRANKENSTEIN

Ralph doesn't recognize the end of summer until a week before school when everyone is running around frantic jumpy shifting gears. He's still operating on summer time even when school starts somehow moving slower than he should it's like he's in slow motion while the world rushes around him. He's not ready to teach he doesn't have course guidelines a syllabus a course reader. He hasn't met with his advisor about the dissertation he doesn't have a plan for the term a schedule deadlines expectations. As far as anyone can tell. Not that they're watching him exactly. And it doesn't bother him being out of sync or it doesn't seem to. He's calm all the time moving

through The Mansion with long loping strides up the stairs down the stairs. He sits in the kitchen a lot drinking coffee reading and reading and reading. Paul doesn't see a pattern in Ralph's books one day Ralph will be reading about electronic technology hypermedia the next day a study of German architecture. His computer's in his room it's where he'd be if he were writing but he's never there except at night. The light in there is usually on until late but what does that mean. Is Ralph working. Paul doesn't know and he wants to. Know. He's fascinated with Ralph lately he admires Ralph's self-structured sense of the world. He wants to know how Ralph does it sets his own course manages time around himself organizes the world. How he stays so calm. Paul wants more and more since living in The Mansion to do that to be like that to be like Ralph. To look like Ralph smiling but focused thoughtful his hair brown and not too long not too short. Wearing a pair of antique frame glasses. Needing a shave but not looking messy he looks like he's taking his time. Deciding if he'll grow a beard.

The Children of Frankenstein

It's for them about control they're at U of F in grad school because they want control. They want control over their lives. Some control to set their own schedules to choose things to study to write to get work done when they want to read write if it's from six to six or from nine to twelve or from twelve to nine or from midnight to three. And they want to work for themselves to get work done for themselves. For themselves. To spend weeks months years on a thing that's ultimately their own. Their papers their stories their dissertations their novels products of their voices their names up at the tops of sheets or on book spines. They want to teach subjects they want to teach

to spend time prepping for class at home a coffee shop in their offices. Wherever. They want to associate with whom they want to associate to not be trapped in a cubicle next to the company wonk. Is it all so much to ask for Paul wonders. It's not like they're asking for money fame power importance they're not even asking for success. Paul thinks. Not exactly. They're only asking for a little bit of freedom. For themselves. That's the problem. Shit Paul thinks what he's thinking could be a Crosby Stills & Nash song. But it's still the bottom line. The Children want a little freedom and that's unFrankensteinian whatever bs about individualism runs through the national consciousness. Almost no one in Frankenstein wants to be an individual actually though all the same people in their same clothes in their same houses with their same attitudes say again and again to themselves and their children the same thing. Just Be Yourself. No. To be from Frankenstein is to understand your duty to family duty to nation duty to community duty to god duty to common values duty to the market employment labor efficiency a work ethic. Well. Paul knows he's being a little simple minded where would we be without some of that. Duty. We'd be in a Mansion without a clean kitchen. Or in Feather's shoes Ralph drives her nuts with his self indulgence a thirty-six-year-old man who behaves like a spoiled child. He does what he wants when he wants and he doesn't justify his actions or even explain them before or after they occur. Everyone else be damned. Where does that leave her where does that leave them Ralph's never going to finish his dissertation he's never going to have a career they're never going to have a family. Or if they're going to have those things she's going to have to make sure they happen and that's not fair. To put it all on her shoulders that fucker. Sometimes Feather wants to walk out the front door and keep on walking. The other day she was making their bed and she wanted to be moving it into a new apartment her own apartment. But she loves him and that's not rational. Is it.

The Children of Frankenstein

Al for one is in control. He doesn't think about control he lives it the way he walks and talks conducts himself. He's got his own agenda don't interfere don't get too close. Al is quiet. Al is observant. Al is aloof he never has still doesn't spend a lot of time hanging around The Mansion except in his room. In the mornings and afternoons and evenings he eats by his own schedule he cleans up after himself he moves from point a to point b with a look of determination and concentration. Evelyn can't remember the last time she saw him lying around the tv room. Maybe he's never done that. His one big contribution to The Mansion he announced in a couple of different ways

and then laid back waiting not pressing. If people would use the livecam they would use the livecam if not not. He hasn't even himself used it not as far as she can tell which really she can't she's never checked the site. But. It's like he's watching and waiting wondering what people might do and where that might lead or maybe it won't lead anywhere. You can't force things. Is what she thinks. But he doesn't come across like a prig not holier than thou aloof but not haughty. When someone interrupts his day catches him in conversation he's always friendly interested. She's noticed that he speaks calmly slowly with concentration. His voice he keeps at a calm reasonable level like he knows that with most people tone is more important than content. She thinks he's probably great with animals he'll be great with children. But because they deserve his respect not because he's a Mr. Rogers. Though she likes Mr. Rogers a whole lot he's a decent man she supposes. She wonders what Al does up in the attic. She's starting to dig the way he looks incredibly tall thin to the point of emaciation long wavy black hair he looks like an orchestra conductor modern music he looks ageless. Could be 24 or 32 or 45.

The Children of Frankenstein

The doorbell doesn't work in The Mansion. There's a tiny round white button outside the front door and a plastic box high up on the wall in the entryway it holds electronic chimes they've figured. But the two don't seem to be connected you can push the button and push the button and no chimes. It's never been a problem except for packages for package delivery but that's not a problem anymore. Nick the mailman and the UPS guy too they know to pound on the door to wait and then pound again. It's too late in the afternoon for either of them though when Cloud hears something downstairs a clacking then a series of cracks and a thump. He's in his room

the only one home as far as he knows. He figures it's PaulAlWindEvelynFeatherRalph coming home Joan won't be back until evening. Maybe they have groceries maybe that's the noise bags of canned goods milk bananas coffee dropping onto the porch then inside on the floor. But Cloud doesn't think he heard the front door open and close he waits a minute then he hears a wunk a scuttle what sounds like scratching a noise it sounds like baba. Then sooky buby nishtgedeit. For a second he believes there are sheep downstairs. Then he thinks maybe a space alien the envoy of an extraterrestrial life chattering in his living room but still he hasn't heard the front door open and close. Maybe they've got very big mice. He puts down his book opens his bedroom door looks out along the hallway. There's nothing there he walks to the head of the stairs the afternoon light is murky it's cloudy outside. There are no lights on in The Mansion just a reading lamp in his room. Hello he asks. Paul. He puts a foot on the top stair starts down. Hello. Al. Two more steps then three four he's trying to see both ways at once up and down the front hallway when he sees a sudden rushing near the tv room something black and huge sliding through the air and all at once he feels like shapes are materializing out of the dimness. Fuck he says he runs back upstairs. Out his bedroom window he sees two kids up the street boxes under their arms. They walk up onto a neighbor's porch ring the bell. They're selling candy.

THE CHILDREN OF FRANKENSTEIN

They believe he saw something but they're not spooked they're full of explanations. They're rational creatures after all it could have been a shadow of a passing truck that cut in front of the afternoon light as it went up the street. It could have been something just outside the windows a squirrel or a bird or several squirrels or several birds fighting nesting. Maybe the noises had been kids knocking on the door. Maybe a neighbor had stopped by maybe it was the owner or his workmen banging things here and there as they stopped by The Mansion. Maybe a paperboy. We don't get the paper Cloud says. Maybe they want us to Evelyn says back. Maybe they were coming by to sell us a subscrip-

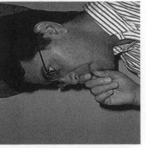

tion. Maybe we do have mice Al says or an animal got inside through the chimney. Maybe it was Sasquatch Paul says. They look at him he grins he says In the time of the animals before men were created a god called Flows-with-the-streaming-clouds was lonely and wanted somebody to talk to. So he created animals who could talk and these animals were something like bears and something like men. They could talk but not through their mouths through their navels they used their mouths for other things like eating and fighting and reproduction. Also they couldn't talk about the kinds of things we talk about because their voices weren't connected with their brains they were connected with their bodies and instead of coming through the windpipe came through the intestines. So they could only talk about what they felt they couldn't talk about what they thought. It's not that they didn't have heads on their shoulders they did but they used them for other things besides thinking like seeing hearing smelling tasting butting and licking you wouldn't believe all the things these guys found to lick he says he waggles his tongue. What they didn't have was necks. But then they didn't need them because they didn't have voice boxes. It's not as if they were stupid they weren't stupid just different. Now these Sasquatch as the Indians call them were very happy. Their words were growls squeaks farts gargles clicks and chuckles Paul stops for a second bjorsq he says they were always jabbering to one another. They were something like bears who have just learned to play the piano. The only trouble was they couldn't learn how to talk to the gods and this made Flows-with-the-streaming-clouds very angry. So he sent the Condors. The what Feather wants to know the Condors. Right Paul says the Condors the ancient Condors now live in the mountains to the east the biggest birds in the world bigger than their South American brothers there are possibly fifty of them left in Frankenstein even now and maybe even on the earth. So he sent the Condors after them and the Condors carried them off by their navels and shook them till their guts ripped and their heads were nearly torn from their bodies and when the Condors were through with them their voices came out of their mouths and they were men.

And that's why men have necks because after the Condors they needed something to keep their heads connected with their bodies. But though men were now able to learn the speech of the gods they always remembered the pain that gift caused them and they weren't happy. And so it turned out that the gods didn't want to talk with them anyway because it was such a down. So Flows-with-the-streaming-clouds ended up as lonely as he was to begin with. And the Indians say there are still some Sasquatch left still hiding from the Condors and sometimes they come out when it's dark murky but that that they're very bitter after all that's happened. Anthropologists consider this a very old myth that may actually represent an unknown stage in the evolution from animal to human some inconceivably subhuman but superanimal species preceding Pithecanthropus Erectus that might have in fact lived at the same time as the Condors which are very ancient. Some species intelligent enough to be free but too dumb to be unhappy. No one really has anything to say to this they all stare at Paul. The Sasquatch he says. The Missing Lunk. I read about it somewhere. Joan's pissed. Cloud's upset after being mugged after all he's clearly still upset and the tension level in The Mansion has been enormous with the start of school and it's set him off. He's seeing things he's frightened. And Paul's blathering on about Sasquatches. It's not funny. She looks around she sees that Al is smiling Wind is too Evelyn looks like she wants to smile Ralph has put his arm around Feather Cloud is staring at Paul. The Missing Lunk Cloud says his narrow and long mostly vertical body hunching in on itself. Bjorsq Paul says back he raises an eyebrow.

THE CHILDREN OF FRANKENSTEIN

She knows better than to be superstitious but Feather is still spooked. And anyway she's not so much superstitious that would be irrational a fear of bogeymen not stepping on cracks. As smart. No not smart sensitive. In tune. Or whatever whatever it's called it's about being aware which just makes good sense to her. Something is going on in The Mansion something with Cloud and if that's the case it doesn't matter if that something comes from a fear of shadows or Sasquatches jangled nerves or a need for attention. If something is going on then something is going on and therefore it's real. Or at least there are effects and effects have to come from somewhere. Or something which is real even if it is imagined if it has effects then the imaginary is no longer just that. What Feather feels is very real she's spooked. Feather is afraid of robbers she's afraid of drug addicts she's afraid of kids who wander up and down in front of The Mansion in fat coats and sneakers. She's afraid of leaving the doors unlocked. Feather is afraid that she's a racist because the people she's afraid of are black. She's afraid that being afraid is ridiculous. She lies awake at night Ralph's light is on Ralph is at his desk. She stares at the cracks in the ceiling the room's trim painted so many times it looks like a bubble snailing along the wall. The closet door and the closet are shadows next to them her shoes her clothes are piled on a chair. Feather is afraid of Terry that he'll come over to The Mansion when no one is around or even if people are around he'll have a beer seem friendly he'll need to use the bathroom. He'll come to the room where she's sleeping Ralph isn't there and she'll wake up and he'll be watching her. And then what. Why wasn't she worried before. Was she.

The Children of Frankenstein

Of them all it's Feather in Paul's viewfinder most often it's Feather. Her pictures don't always make it on to The Children's homepage but again and again Paul's camera points at Feather. In our art as in our lives is what Paul tells himself when he notices what he's doing is what everyone does when faced with Feather. Stare. If at all possible it can't be helped she's stunning voluptuous only the right curves softness her face finely featured freckles over the bridge of her nose her hair blond curly. She's their very own Venus she's gorgeous she draws the eye. Paul likes her best when she smiles she smiles a lot.

The Children of Frankenstein

A visit from Terry. Terry comes across his yard when he sees them inspecting the outside of The Mansion they're looking for forced windows jimmied locks. He pretends he's wandering over in the interests of being neighborly but that's not why he comes over. Terry comes over because he's sensitized to trouble like a police dog to pot. Evelyn thinks. He likes trouble it's entertainment for him especially if it involves college kids. Not college kids exactly but middle-class kids. Not middle-class kids exactly but the entire middle class he wants them to suffer for what they have who they are. He wants them to experience the kind of hardships he's experienced manual labor

eight hours a day five days a week twenty years of smashing his knuckles on the insides of cars grease all over himself it never comes off. Fucking customers with their Jap cars. Dickhead boss. How's it hangin he asks Cloud. Hanging Cloud says not a question exactly. He looks at Terry. Checking your storms Terry asks then laughs. There aren't any storm windows on The Mansion there aren't even screens. Right Feather says weatherproofing smiles he turns toward her not smiling. Actually we're checking for signs of entry Ralph says someone might have gotten in the other day. Uhhuh. Terry. Like he already knows. Kids in here before you forgot to lock their doors. They got scared after someone ripped 'em off. Wind wants to tell Terry they already know he already told them this but he finds himself staring at Terry's boots black and scuffed only the tips still have shape. Steel toes he thinks he wonders how many years old they are. The boots. Evelyn thinks that for Terry trouble isn't even entertainment it's a seam into which he can insert himself a gap an aporia a space opening up where there wasn't one before. Why would he want to do that. What can a person get out of being involved in an uncertain situation confusion. What's to be had. Presence what comes with presence. Attention. Maybe. It's what Evelyn gets with presence people notice her. It seems like they wouldn't she's not a lot of presence dark and small thin arms and legs her fine hair pulled behind her ears. But Evelyn's fierce concentrated energy always her face shows this in a serious serious look an intense focus. People see her when she's around. Feather says hey. Oh no. The wind chimes her wind chimes they're all gone. Al finds a few pieces some chimes on the ground by the garden but that's it. That's all.

The Children of Frankenstein

It occurs to Paul to check in the basement to check on his grow lamps his irrigation beds his plants. If someone's been in the house then maybe someone's seen his setup. It makes him nervous. It also makes him nervous that JoanCloudAlWindEvelynFeatherorRalph might think to do the same as him scout around downstairs looking for signs of entry so he does it first volunteers makes sure everyone knows his intentions. No one's gone down in the basement in a while not in the back where he's got the setup. Why would they it's not time for winter gardening they've still got everything they want in terms of veggies flowers herbs in the backyard. Paul's got the grow

lamps on a trip switch they flick off when the basement door opens. That wouldn't stop anyone from doing what people normally do in the basement though pull the chains on the overhead bulbs before wandering around. The overheads would cast enough light for them to see. His plants. They're hard to miss they'd be hard to miss if anyone scouted around a little there are six of them over five feet tall they've got leaves the size of dinner plates. It's not his first crop it's his second. The first was experimental a learning phase it didn't produce much he didn't know how to prune the plants he snipped some buds too early some too late he let a male plant survive and got in the entire harvest seeds seeds and more seeds. Which he's read are useless homegrown loses potency after one breeding the seeds would produce impotent buds. Oh well. The entire first crop only took a month and a half hydroponics are wickedly efficient and it left him some smokeables while he started in on the second. Crop. From fresh seeds. He thinks he might sell some this time around he needs to recoup costs. He's been intercepting the electric bill it's in his name after all he's been paying for the lights no one knows. And his digital camera. It was on sale but it wasn't cheap. He'll sell enough to pay for these things and not more and he's looking for trouble. He knows people who can use a little spliff. He'll only sell to friends not Mansion friends. He'll never say where the stuff comes from. Everything in the basement looks fine. The smell Paul notices is strong it's musky earthy sharp. Green. This worries him. And pretty soon people FeatherAlRalphEvelynCloud JoanorWind might want to start using the rig for winter veggies the backyard garden will reach the end of its life. This worries him. He doesn't want to get caught to get in trouble.

The Children of Frankenstein

It's fine Anny insists they need some time apart. Not time apart time apart. But now and then like tonight a night away from each other. Who doesn't she asks Ralph. Need their own space sometimes. You know what I mean. A little breathing space elbow room she tells him. Right. God I love this house she says she's staying over. She's had too much to drink she and Feather have polished off almost two bottles of wine. Ralph's had a little he decided a glass was in order when he saw how much they were drinking he figures what goes into him doesn't go into them. What doesn't go into them doesn't increase their volume. Ralph pictures Paul trying to watch tv Joan and Cloud

trying to sleep. He'd be more than happy to drive Anny home it's no bother. This is out of the question how will she get her car tomorrow Feather asks why doesn't she just stay over here. He's afraid I'm going to kick him out of his bed Anny says that the girls will take over the bedroom and he'll have to sleep on the sofa. Look at him she yells look at his face I'm right which Feather finds funny she's amused. Ha. Ha. Ha. Ralph hadn't thought this no one ever asks him to give up his bed unexpectedly it's not the kind of thing people ask him to do. Or not the kind of thing people have asked him to do in what. A decade almost. And anyway who says Feather would want to share a bed with a friend that's weird Ralph thinks though maybe less weird for women than for men because of cultural conditioning he thinks. Slumber parties when they're younger girls in their nighties doing each other's hair a kind of nonsexual communal feeling snuggling up next to whoever's closest. Or is this just a male vision of slumber parties a pedophiliac fantasy. This is what Ralph is thinking what registers on his face he supposes. Feather and Anny watch him for a second they burst out laughing. Again. He smiles puts on his game face. Stands up he says he's going to watch tv with Paul Anny says no we're just teasing. But he notices that that's all she says Feather doesn't say anything. When he's down the hall he hears them laughing again. In the tv room he sits down. Hey he says. Hey Paul says. He doesn't turn to look at Ralph. Sounds like fun eh.

The Children of Frankenstein

Ralph's got a pretty good sense of humor he thinks. Most of the time. When he's on the same wavelength as who he's joking with when they're both getting what they're supposed to get. In terms of the joke. But he's not sure with Anny. When she's joking because she thinks she's funny when she's half-joking she's not sure about how she'll be received when she's joking because she's dead serious angry. Or what. He doesn't know. So he goes to bed without saying goodnight maybe Anny was kidding maybe she wasn't whatever. It won't make a difference if he's in bed asleep when the time comes for Feather and Anny to be in bed asleep. He can't offer up his half of

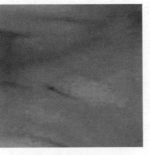

the mattress if he's already on it dead to the world. Which he supposes is a selfish attitude definitely not chivalrous so what. He's too old to let anyone keep him from a good night's sleep. He's not in the mood even to give more than a second's idle thought to the erotic possibilities of two drunk women in bed to the possibility of him in between two drunk women in bed. He just gets into bed he falls asleep. When he wakes up it's pitch dark someone is kissing him it's a she she smells like wine she feels warm soft. It's odd but he thinks he sees a blue glow around her head Feather he says she doesn't say anything back she takes his cock in one hand moves down kisses its tip. Feather he says she says I'll be right back she's up and out the door. She comes into the room again in a minute or two or maybe five Ralph wonders if she's not well if she went to throw up she says she's okay she puts her arms around him. When he leans into her she's willing if not as ready or able as before. The blue glow around her head Ralph notices is gone.

THE CHILDREN OF FRANKENSTEIN

Paul's finally getting some. Who knows how long it's been since he last had sex he's not got sex appeal he's like a teddy bear short and brown he's cute he's huggable not fuckable. But now. He was minding his business watching the tube when in came Anny and suddenly a little boom boom. She didn't say anything he didn't say anything after a second they were tangled together they moved to his room where they get it on. Is all Paul can think as it happens he finds the phrase stuck in his head as he pumps into Anny. Gettin' it on gettin' it on gettin' it on gettin' it on gettin' it on gettin' it on gettin' it on gettin' it on gettin' it on. Paul had been smoking a

little dope before. When they're done he tells her she comes like a tidal wave and she explains how they used to work on perfecting their orgasms she and a former lover orgasm is the closest we come to union with the cosmos orgasm and meditation and death she says she'll have to teach him how to do it. Then he lights up a joint passes it to her and they do it again and after that a third time and then Paul starts to worry that Ralph and Feather will hear. Him and Anny. Her having had a lot to drink. She's married. Feather wouldn't be happy he doesn't want Ralph to hear he'd tell Feather. Paul's sure not going to say anything to anybody he doesn't have to ask Anny he knows she won't either. Finally getting some. Gettin' it on.

The Children of Frankenstein

Wind's not gettin it on he's not going to be gettin anything on anymore. Is what he figures. Evelyn's not in the mood she hasn't been in the mood since school started is not going to be in the mood while the semester is in session. She gets uptight when under pressure and school makes her feel under pressure. Nights she gets awful backaches from the stress her muscles bind into tight knobs. Most nights. Wind wakes up to find her flopped forward over her legs stretched in half it's like she's touching her toes in her sleep. It loosens her back she says when she's awake she doesn't know she's doing it half the time. She's a sleep contortionist Wind thinks. How can someone

limber enough to touch her toes in her sleep have muscle problems backaches. It's where she carries her tension she says. She carries it in her thighs too Wind thinks in his less generous moments she doesn't want him between them. When he's between them they seem constricted like they're trying to push him out. It makes him feel like he's forcing her when they have sex it makes him feel like a rapist as if she says she's willing but really she's not. It makes him want not so much to get it on as get it over with. Wind's felt limp lately it's frustrating he's frustrated. Not having sex not wanting to have sex makes him want to jump off a cliff. Or sleep he feels like an important part of his life has gone missing awol. Or maybe it's just situation normal all fucked up. Or that things are fucked up beyond all recognition. Awol snafu fubar. Worst of all he feels like a jerk for feeling frustrated he tries to see things from her point of view she's unhappy under pressure not in the mood. But how empathetic should a person be. If you're not getting what you want because someone else is aren't you a sucker a schmuck a schnook a wonk a wiener a tool. And she's such a bitch lately. Not just to him but about everyone. He likes CloudJoanRalphFeatherAlandPaul he feels bad when she criticizes them. He thinks she feels bad criticizing but she can't seem to stop herself.

THE CHILDREN OF FRANKENSTEIN

Evelyn feels bad criticizing CloudJoanRalphFeatherAlandPaul which she's doing more and more lately in her own head and to Wind. But she just can't help herself Feather emoting all over the place wanting love comfort solace in the face of what's just another semester isn't it. Ralph walking around with a stick in his butt it seems like he gets more and more self righteously self involved when anything's asked of him when the normal demands of life start to intrude he becomes a completely humorless bastard she thinks. Joan roaming The Mansion like their own spectral presence not saying much to anyone but gliding from room to room with a book in her hand always

looking lost in thought preoccupied she should be wearing a long white shift Evelyn thinks and levitating gliding along instead of actually using her feet. Ghostly. Ghastly. Cloud's been twitchy nervous panicky about something and instead of carrying it in himself he's been ramming it down everyone's throats by trying to be funny. The unhappier he gets the funnier he thinks he is the funnier he thinks he is the more he starts performing. He becomes a clown he makes a character out of himself a caricature. There's a fear in it all Evelyn thinks a fear she thinks she understands a terror of being soft. You have to be hard as hard as whatever it is that hurts you. You have to become what hurts you. Or else. Or else it may hurt you again. This bothers her. When you turn hard you move out of contact. And Paul's stoned all the time hasn't anyone else noticed. She wonders how he can afford the dope. At least he keeps to himself. Like Al who she finds she likes maybe because she doesn't know the first thing about him really what a relief. Not knowing is easier it's a way of evading things people life but so what she's supposed to embrace everything is she supposed to let Wind into her every time he feels a twitch in his dick.

The Children of Frankenstein

Feather thinks that graduate students make for rotten people rotten friends. No she doesn't think this not really. Not really. But she does she feels like the grad student mindframe the kind of thought processes that make for good scholars can be personally trying frustrating unhappy making. It can lead she thinks to people constantly interrogating analyzing speculating arguing indulging a kind of faithlessness that make them concoct the most outrageous narratives and believe they're real. If they make a certain kind of persuasive sense. All of this all the time during the school year in the past month or so it's as if a switch clicked in The Mansion and suddenly everyone

is ON. It's as if no one can tell the difference anymore between life outside of school and school. School mode bleeds over into everything and Feather can't say the most innocent thing without being questioned quizzed corrected. Feather needs for people to accept understand forgive each other at least some of the time to maybe even listen to each other without listening to words but what their friends are saying in between their words what they're feeling. Not really no not really she doesn't want that she actually finds that sort of attention a kind of inattention doesn't she. She's just like everyone else a graduate student with the same qualities maybe she doesn't like these things in herself. Maybe she's projecting her own self-loathing onto CloudJoanRalphEvelynAlandPaul maybe they're the same as they ever were maybe she's the twitch anymore. Or maybe they have changed. Really. What did she used to think they were. She is just like everyone else she's a graduate student with the same qualities. Isn't she.

THE CHILDREN OF FRANKENSTEIN

What makes Joan edgy is having Feather and Wind in her classes one in one one in the other. Edgy not irritated angry not annoyed. Edgy. As in nervous on the edge of something a steep drop. Off of what. Why. She likes Feather she likes Wind she's been in classes with them before she's been in classes with everyone in The Mansion. It's never been a problem why would it have been. She didn't live with any of them before now she does. With Feather. With Wind. And she's not sure how she's going to deal with them not sure she can deal with them in their newly multiple capacities. Making sense of people understanding them knowing who they are what they're about what they need what they want is hard enough. Hard enough when when you've only got certain factors to consider. Where they're from where they're going what they're going what they do what they like what they don't. Their favorite kinds of food. What for them is taboo how to pique their interests. Everything's harder when you live with them you have to know these things and also their irrationalities their eccentricities when they like to shower eat study relax. When they like to watch their favorite programs. Now Joan's got to contend with Feather and Wind in these ways and as students her peers in her classes. She'll have to come to terms with what they think of the professors the material they'll probably want to share thoughts. They're going to want to swap notes share secondary materials Wind has already asked to borrow one of her books. On the one hand Joan likes to talk she likes interacting with people they provide her with energy she feeds off it. She likes to talk about ideas about literature about philosophy. But she likes to talk about these things in the abstract which leads to the other hand she doesn't like to talk so much about her own ideas about literature philosophy about her own academic work. Not classwork. Not with her friends. Not in her home. Then everything gets too complicated. Joan reserves a place in her brain for schoolwork a private spot into which nothing else can intrude. Until now she's had a corresponding area in her life places and periods of isolation in which she could work. She's afraid she can't function without them both she's afraid that if she insists upon them she'll alienate her friends she's afraid that her friends aren't her friends anymore anyway they're her colleagues. Her competition. They're working for grades aren't they they're all trying to be the best students in the class. Aren't they they're trying to impress the professors to stand out excel. They want the best faculty to work with them. Joan's afraid of what Feather and Wind will come to think of her as the semester proceeds that she can be a real hard ass a gunner a shark. They wouldn't be the first.

The Children of Frankenstein

Paul understands he says. About colliding worlds. He says he feels a little watched lately like everyone in The Mansion's charting their lives their work their progress against his. Not on a conscious level it's like they're casting sideways glances at how much he works how much he reads writes the time he spends on teaching or his dissertation. If I'm doing more than they are he says they must not be doing enough. If I'm doing less they're on the right track. Joan thinks Paul is describing her. I think I do that she says. Everyone does he says. I do it too. I think. To everyone else. It's creepy your entire life is suddenly under observation. It's our version of keeping up with the Joneses

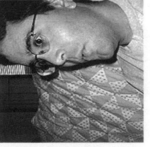

he says. Or something. The experience adds a whole new dimension to eating breakfast. You linger a little too long over your cereal suddenly it feels like everyone's noticing you've lingered too long over your cereal. If you're lingering over your cereal you're not working. It's all part of the equation. Joan suspects Paul is touchy about this because he still watches as much tv as he ever did new semester or no new semester. It's a big part of his equation people do notice. Maybe Paul's insecure about the math people are doing in their heads maybe he feels like they all feel like they're doing more than he is maybe they are. Paul's watching himself by watching other people watch him. I just feel everybody's presence she says. It's not exactly that anybody's watching me but that they're around me. I can't not hear their voices when I'm in The Mansion. Even if nobody's talking. It's like everyone's gotten in my head and they're crowding it up. And that's bad Paul asks. Joan doesn't know. What she knows is that one day recently she saw an expression crossing Wind's face an expression of pain peculiar to Ralph. Then another time she noticed Evelyn's look of subliminal annoyance and had to remind herself that she was talking to Feather. Once she caught Paul laughing like she herself laughs and since then she's been seeing this phenomenon all the time Evelyn's pensive look on her own face Evelyn glowing with excitement like Feather her own smile on Evelyn's lips. When this kind of thing passes between Paul and Wind they look almost like twins they're both small and dark to begin with. They're all at least in part becoming composites of one another she says this to Paul and when this goes on for a while what remains unique to each. Already they have similar backgrounds they have similar interests they speak the same language they do the same kind of work. They've begun to schedule their lives their work by each other's lives each other's work. And now they're inside each other's heads what remains unique to each. Paul thinks maybe it's a rhythm and maybe a quality of response. The way he differs from his father for example or his sister. He thinks maybe all the horizontal things are interchangeable and the vertical ones unique so that for example you might get people behaving the same way again and again and always for different reasons. Does that make sense. He thinks the vertical is like an elevator people go up and down according to temperament. As they go down people make some kind of choice about where they want to get off. The further down you go the fewer the stops and Paul thinks that if you go down far enough there are no more stops at all and then you just keep going down and down and you can't stop. And then what. Bjorsq Joan asks.

The Children of Frankenstein

The thing with Paul is that he likes it when worlds collide. He digs it. He's got a thing against borders he likes when they disintegrate. He feels this way even though he knows that when things break down there are problems he has problems. He breaks down when he starts to be unsure of who's who when he doesn't know whose voice is whose other people's voices in his head mixing with sometimes passing for his own. When he doesn't know where one thing ends school for example and another begins life in The Mansion and that's just one example. When this starts to make it impossible for him to tell the difference between one thing and another. When he doesn't know in other words up

from down or out from in when each time he enters one thing from another from The Mansion to school to his personal life to school to his personal life to The Mansion there seems to be less and less any outside around. But he likes the confusion he needs it it complicates things. It helps him break away from set ideas assumptions it opens things up. It helps make traditional conventional fixed boring methods of doing things impossible the confusion points him toward what he thinks of as the ultimate chaos in life. That there's no plot. It also helps him come to see on a day to day basis in little flashes that if there's no plot in the chaos of life then no meaning preexists his experiences or his interpretations of his experiences and meaning is produced in the process of living and reading and writing. What this means in the long view is that he doesn't need necessarily to see everything around him as being meaningful truthful realistic he doesn't have to see his world as a vehicle for ready made meanings. Wow. The whole scenario can sometimes scare the shit out of him because taken all together it suggests that his experiences exist only as fiction that most fiction is more or less based on the experiences of the one who makes it and that there cannot be any truth nor any reality exterior to fiction. Thinking about this tends to make Paul dizzy. Paul's biggest fear is that he'll crack up if when the world begins to disintegrate around him he'll become loopy. That might be outside of fictions maybe the only thing that is. This is why Paul gets nervous when he begins to sense the possibility of a breach terrified that he'll become frayed susceptible to an unwinding a spin into multiple threads multiple directions. What he tells Joan is that at one point in his life before he knew her I guess I had some kind of break down. Or break up. Or break through. I had too much going on inside me the pressure was too much. I sort of broke open. I was kind of a bundle of parts that didn't go together any more. I'm better now he says I'm back together again I'm keeping it together. He laughs he thinks she thinks its funny when he uses the language the phrases of another generation. He doesn't know what else she thinks about him. He's pretty sure she doesn't know what he thinks about her how he feels about her that he's in love with her. He's begun to wish that Cloud were out of the picture. Really.

THE CHILDREN OF FRANKENSTEIN

Cloud's not doing dishes his plates his forks knives spoons his bowls his glasses his mugs all pile up in the sink beside the sink on the counter. The kitchen's a mess a lot it's mostly Cloud's fault. He doesn't have time or he doesn't want to be bothered at least not right after eating by chores tasks by soaping scrubbing rinsing drying. By putting things away. First things first Cloud's got work to do he's got a chapter due he's got books to read he's got email to write he's got to keep his focus. Cloud's got a thing about focus he thinks that if he keeps his mind at all times one way or another turned toward one end his project his ideas then he's focussed he's devoting his every available energy to a specific goal. Any time

away from that goal is wasted time procrastinating a diversion and who knows what work he might have gotten done in that time what book he might have been able to start reading finish reading what notes he might have been able to take what great ideas might have emerged. But didn't and so are lost. For good. What Cloud won't admit to himself can't admit to himself he thinks he's a logical man a competent grown up. Is that his attitude is fundamentally illogical he's superstitious not washing dishes is the same as not stepping on a crack. Step on a crack you'll break your. Concentration. Do one thing take the same steps follow the same routine day in and day out and you'll be okay. Okay. Okay. Cloud's taken to staying up until all hours when Evelyn wanders out in the middle of the night she needs to use the bathroom Cloud's at the bottom of the stairs. At three a.m. when Wind goes for a glass of water Cloud's got his head in the fridge. Joan he shocks out of sleep he comes into their bedroom and goes out again comes in again heads out again always every night bumbling in the dark for things from his desk for a clean pair of socks a sweater. What bothers Feather most about Cloud is the physical reality of his presence it's one big jitter. She sometimes imagines that she can see Cloud thrumming with some high pitched vibration keening to something that he and only he can hear and when she's around him long enough she feels in her nerves a sympathetic trembling. And she doesn't need that it interferes with her sleep her concentration she's got enough trouble. What's his problem. Paul thinks that Cloud has too much time on his hands that he can only write for so many hours a day and the rest of his time is taken up with thinking about writing but more generally just turning things around in his head he may be going a little crazy. Paul thinks Cloud has too much imagination and too much time to indulge it and too little control over it. There's no order in his life no routine. And all this time thinking with nothing for his body to do of course it's going to be twitchy restless he has all sorts of feelings in his body and all sorts of ideas in his head and he doesn't know how to bring them together. He doesn't know what to do with himself. Paul wouldn't be surprised if Cloud's most of the time got a tremendous pain in the neck. After all the neck is what's in between the head and the body.

The Children of Frankenstein

Wind comes to the conclusion that Cloud is a lazy sack of shit he conjures up any rationale he can for not doing his share of the communal work keeping The Mansion habitable livable clean bug roach mouse free. Of all the people to not have enough time to do dishes. Cloud's on fellowship for Christ's sake he doesn't have to teach he doesn't have to cater he doesn't have any more classes. Nothing. The other day he tells Paul there wasn't even enough space in the sink so that I could do my dishes. I was this close to going upstairs and hauling him down by the scruff of his neck. I was going to make him wash every dish I could find. Paul doesn't say anything

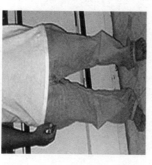

he doesn't think that Wind is big enough to haul anybody around neither is he. But then again. At the very least Wind says I wanted to give him a sharp whack on the back of the head. A good smack he says to Paul's surprised look. Paul says. Wow. Nyuck Nyuck Nyuck. Woowoowoowoowoowoowoowoo. Paul wants to say they're just dishes.

The Children of Frankenstein

Ralph grew up with a sister a mother he's seen feminine hygiene items tampons sanitary napkins he's seen them used and not. This though is unlike anything Ralph has ever seen the garbage in the upstairs bathroom it's heaped with folded bloody napkins with cardboard applicators tampons half in their pink disposal bags. The garbage is stuffed it's overflowing with wads in different shades of red covered in some cases with what he can see from the door to be chunky mucus he's not a squeamish man but. He can't imagine so much blood all at once flowing within the walls of The Mansion he doesn't understand. Not one not two only maybe three women menstru-

ating at the same time could produce this kind of waste he can't believe no one has taken out the garbage. He's not going to he's not even going to use the upstairs bathroom. So what's new. If it's not one thing it's another. Lately it's been Evelyn she's been hogging the bathroom taking baths almost every night of the past week the past two weeks she cranks on the faucets the hot a lot the cold a little the upstairs tub is an ancient enormous ceramic stand alone with clawed feet. While the tub fills she sits in the bathroom staring at nothing as the room starts to fill with steam she takes off her clothes slowly a piece at a time starting with her socks then her pants after a few minutes her sweater. Then her shirt when the tub is almost full her bra and just before she slips in and under the surface the air cold enough and the water hot enough that wisps of steam curl off the water's surface she takes off her panties. Evelyn goes into the tub in one motion carefully so she doesn't slip but in one motion it's painful at first not a little painful it hurts hurts. But she likes it it's a good pain Evelyn likes cankers that she can dig at with her tongue she likes flossing her teeth a little too hard nagging the gums until they bleed she likes scabs peeling them off slowly a millimeter at a time. Evelyn likes the feel of a knife razor sharp or a razor razor sharp running down cutting through the soft upper part of her arm the inside of her thigh. Wrong. Evelyn used to like that. She doesn't anymore she won't let herself anymore she can't wear shirts with short sleeves she can't wear shorts that come too high above her knee and anyway what a cliché. Self-mutilation. She likes baths hot baths. Really hot baths. Evelyn can't turn off she's tense because she can't. She wakes up in the morning tired. Her dreams are long complicated affairs that she can never remember she just remembers having them all night long. She doesn't drift in and out of them she's always having them is what she thinks and she wakes up tired an edgy tired she's thinking the minute her eyes open she's thinking as she gets out of bed she's alert but not in a thoughtful way. Alert like a rabbit. In headlights jumpy everything around her registers she can't shut anything out she can't turn herself off not in the morning not in the afternoon not in the evening. Everything registers she hears everything around her she sees everything around her and everything has meaning. She thinks. She can't stop thinking. It makes her a good student. But she can't control it she thinks about her work but also about what Cloud said or what Paul said or how Feather reacted to what she Evelyn said or Wind his behavior. She thinks about the future whatever she thinks about she has to find some meaning in it makes her hard to be around she wants people to like her to love her but she stares at people she doesn't trust what they say not on the surface at least she's tired tense irritable angry. Evelyn can't be angry at other people but she's angry. Evelyn's angry she's been angry a lot in her life she can't be angry at other people. Evelyn would like to slice her skin open she would like to measure out the cut the pain then watch the skin flap back together again there's never much blood. She'd like to injure herself. She doesn't. After a while in the bath the anger leaches out she's wrung out she's tired finally tired. When Ralph knocks on the door it doesn't even register she doesn't say anything she doesn't move not even when he comes in stutters and goes back out again. When Wind asks she says that baths relax her muscles.

THE CHILDREN OF FRANKENSTEIN

No one believes it when Joan yells at Wind they're usually very civil to each other the two people in The Mansion with the least casual relationship. August thinks that you have to know someone pretty well that you have to be comfortable with a person before you can yell at him. Or her but this. What. No one knows they just hear Joan shouting in the kitchen. And then Wind is out the door he doesn't say anything he's going running it's what he does he's run for ten years three or four times a week three or four miles at a stretch he can't not run. He eats breathes sleeps craps runs they're all necessary body functions he can no more stop running than he can stop

anything else his body needs he believes this he believes this he has to run. Wind has to run more when he's upset when Joan yells at him for example he needs a change in rhythm in function in metabolism for his body to move into a different pace slower where his brain wakes up not into rational thought but another kind. His ideas emerge in time with his feet which present themselves in front of him one then the other then the other then the other and they never move out of control the feet the ideas because he never stays with one for any length of time. He just sees them a foot an idea and then they're gone and then they're back. But different. For one two three four five six seven eight nine ten eleven twelve thirteen fourteen fifteen sixteen seventeen eighteen nineteen minutes he thinks he has to go to the library in the afternoon he has a chapter to read tonight he'll have to get up early tomorrow he wants to catch a shower before Feather she's been a little jumpy lately she's been quiet too. Is it The Mansion what's the problem. Paul's been quiet too in a reverie. Ralph Ralph Ralph's a little chafed lately bothered but not ruffled. But bothered. By what what's bothering Ralph. Maybe it's Cloud. Cloud. Cloud he's going to wring Cloud's neck. No. No. Cloud is just being Cloud he's Wind's annoying too he imagines he thinks. In his own way which is. What. Evelyn. And her baths. When she gets out of them when she comes to bed her skin is hot. It's so hot it makes his cock spring up. Evelyn. Evelyn. She doesn't want to be touched. And Al. What about Al. What about Al after three miles after thirty minutes Wind is empty emptied out not tired but not altogether in himself anymore not there nothing much no thought at all he just feels his calves his thighs his heels they're there his body he feels them. For another half mile or a mile he slows down he winds down he stops. He stretches again. He's on the grass at a park he's by the lake it's fall but still warm the sun is out it's not hot but not not he feels a chill. Something blocks the sun something black and huge sliding through the air way up perfectly still sliding through the air then it's gone.

The Children of Frankenstein

Everyone's surprised when Paul springs for cable he doesn't ask if anyone in The Mansion wants it he doesn't ask anyone to pitch in. One day there's cable. The next there's another tv in Paul's room Paul goes into the basement he splices the cable now one branch runs into his bedroom he's got an illegal cable box in there. He bought it online. Sometimes when Joan's outside at night she walks along the side of the house. If she looks toward Paul's room it's dark but lit up with blue and green flashes sometimes brighter flashes white. But mostly blue and green she thinks it looks like a battlezone in the deepest jungle tracers and exploding shells.

The Children of Frankenstein

Joan doesn't know. Maybe they're all friends in The Mansion maybe they aren't. She doesn't know. She knew when they moved into The Mansion that they weren't they didn't know each other really or at least not well how could they be friends but then. But then it seemed there was more than that something more she thinks. She knows she didn't much question things life in The Mansion just felt good right. Right. How unlike her to just accept it. How she feels now this is more like her she more often than she can handle feels buttery uncertain she can't walk in the front door without feeling something in her stomach. She can't walk down the hall and not be nervous even jumpy nervous weak nervous fragile at those moments if something someone were to startle her she would shrink fall curl onto the floor. Is how she feels and when she feels like this and she talks to AlPaulEvelynRalph FeatherevenCloud she finds herself rattling she can't control her thoughts. The less she can control her thoughts the more she talks the less she knows what she's saying the faster she says what. Whatever. Who knows. Joan doesn't she doesn't know. She used to know ———— was a friend they had friends in common they hung out they talked they drank they smoked this is what they did all of them they did it in bars in apartments in her room ———— was the last one to leave they were drinking they were talking she was asleep. Then she wasn't she was awake but drunk she was gagging. _____ was pushing his cock into her mouth she couldn't breathe to say no she couldn't breathe she tried to shake her head no to shake his cock out but she couldn't he came in her mouth onto her face she said no she thinks she doesn't know if she said no. She did but it didn't seem to mean anything it didn't work she was afraid ashamed embarrassed she didn't say anything else she didn't scream. She knows he spread her legs her muscles felt useless frightened atrophied she was scared tense scared panicked and limp dysfunctional he pushed into her he kept her on her back her arms over her head he had a hand around her throat she felt wet but it couldn't be he kept fucking her when he turned her onto her stomach she saw blood on his cock she wanted to vomit. He seemed angry furious what did she do what could she do he wouldn't leave he kept fucking her. She never told anyone no one knows not then not now not Cloud. _____ was her friend. Wasn't he. How could she how can she know Joan just doesn't know.

The Children of Frankenstein

Al knows what he needs he needs clarity. He knows he can't have it not absolute clarity there's no way to fix a moment people in time and space to understand fully everything there is to understand about them. But he wants it so he does what he can to work toward it. Mostly what he does is avoid people their complications their confusions the ways they overwhelm themselves each other him. If Al has to confront people he tries to do so on his own terms they're less slippery then when he can set the rules of engagement when he knows the starting points of their conversations the ending points the subjects to be discussed. There's less disorder that way no un-

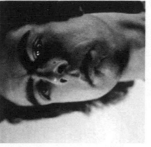

charted territory to slip into to find he's in over his head that he's exceeded his grasp no times when he finds himself bound up in subtle transformations of conversation of rules of friendships relationships transformations that he doesn't understand until after the fact. No. Not that. Karen though Karen's an exception for now at least she's a good confusion she gives him a rise. In a good way she's beyond him bigger more. She's smarter than he is she's got a plan. He's a small part in her life he's not sure what that part is she always keeps him guessing. He never knows what she's up to where he fits into her life her story what's his role. She's in and out of The Mansion his days his weeks his life on who knows what schedule. Al doesn't know what will happen when Karen comes around two weeks ago a conversation that's all talk about U of F The Mansion they had drinks. Last week no talking Karen came into the attic and curled up in his bed hugged a pillow. Tonight she's got on thigh-high vinyl boots and nothing else she commands him to kneel to close his eyes after a minute he feels her hand in his hair she pulls his head up he flinches when something stings lightly across his back he opens his eyes. A riding crop. Cool he thinks he's told to shut his fucking eyes. What Al knows he doesn't want is a party in The Mansion he can't handle that kind of chaos. But Al can't say this he can't tell anyone how he feels. He can't handle an argument.

The Children of Frankenstein

The party was Feather's idea. In a way. She was straightening the kitchen when Evelyn came in Feather reached up putting away dishes she said Hey don't you think it's time for a party. She looked from between her raised arms her cheeks freckled smiling her hair red-gold in the afternoon sun. A party said Evelyn it's funny but I've been thinking that too we need to do something together something fun. They finished the kitchen went to the living room where Paul lay stretched on the sofa reading watching tv he took them both in as they stood watching him his eyes wide What he said What's wrong. Then before they could say anything he said You know I've

been wondering if we ought to have a party. When Wind came home found them all three in front of the tv talking he stopped he said You're planning a party. Right. Ralph turned to Cloud later almost bumping into him in the hall sounds of talk from downstairs said they're planning a party that's what I thought said Cloud That makes sense later telling Joan when she crawled into bed. Oh. She said. Oh.

THE CHILDREN OF FRANKENSTEIN

They'll invite graduate students and their significant others their spouses they'll invite their friends from catering they'll even invite some of the faculty. And their significant others their spouses. They'll chip in they'll get a keg wine some hard stuff. For food they'll make it a potluck everyone will bring some food. A Potlatch Paul says but the name doesn't stick. A potluck. They'll each make something too an appetizer a main dish a dessert. Feather's set on dessert she'll make a cake something complicated from her Cake Bible. She's worried the oven won't work it'll be too hot too cold uneven. Ralph says he's going to make pizzas everything from scratch the dough the

sauce tomatoes from the garden the toppings he'll get from the garden the very last of the final pickings green peppers onions. How about a string bean pizza Cloud asks how about putting corn on one he's in charge of getting chips. The dip Paul will make. Sour cream mixed with french onion soup mix guacamole an authentic version fresh avocados tomatoes onions. Salsa from a jar Paul's got no facility for making salsa he's tried before it always ends up ketchup. Wind will make a lasagna he's the king of lasagna he can make eggplant parmigiana too if it's put together like a lasagna he can handle those sorts of dishes. They don't have to be finessed they're just ingredients layered onto ingredients layered onto ingredients layered onto ingredients lots of cheese sauce nothing subtle about it all baked into a satisfying conglomeration a whole enormous pan of food is what Wind's going to make. It's the kind of thing Wind makes all the time on Sundays and stretches the entire week. For himself and Evelyn. Evelyn's going to make scones she's not sure how they'll fit with everything else but it's what she knows how to make the only thing she ever makes she likes them with her coffee. Joan's in charge of drinks she'll take the beverage money and buy soda wine when it's time for the keg Cloud's going to drive her in his minivan. She's going to make a punch too juice with a little champagne very festive. Their guests they figure will bring standard potluck fare bean dishes assorted casseroles salads fruit bowls bread veggies desserts they'll bring booze even if they're told they don't have to bottles of wine six-packs of beer maybe someone will bring a bottle of tequila and a bag of limes. What about Al.

THE CHILDREN OF FRANKENSTEIN

Al thinks that whatever else they may be The Children of Frankenstein are creatures of context pragmatists they adapt to their surroundings. What others do they do life's a matter of community. Their parents were creatures of biology and chance or so they thought. They thought they could work through or with biology and chance by using imagination they figured they should have enough imagination to deal with their particular allotments of biology and chance. That was their standard when they imagined a standard. Only they forgot that when you imagine a standard you get a standard imagination this is what they ended up with most of them a sense of the horizontal

a horizontal sense. This is what they finally taught their children. What others do they do life's a matter of community they figure out the rules games and then play by them. Only life's not a game Al thinks at least after a certain point on a certain level he's sure that the other Children realize this too they've all been in contexts where the game's not fun it's got built into it a what. Al doesn't know he can't say reality quotient because all games are the realities of their particular moments their own realities but there's something more. Something else. Something scary. What. It depends. Al thinks that beyond the present context The Children's lives aren't theirs. They've lost touch with who they are or have to be in situations other than the one in which they're living now. He's afraid that PaulWindEvelynRalph CloudFeatherandJoan have lost sight of this this this makes him very edgy. He thinks a party will be a complete disaster. He can't say this to anyone. He can't not go. He thinks his being there is fated. Why this is isn't clear. He tells Feather that for the big event he'll make a mulligan stew. Why not. It's something he's never made he's never even eaten it's not his kind of food. It's the perfect choice.

The Children of Frankenstein

Paul asks that during the party no one be shown the hydroponics equipment it's not set up he says maybe no one should mention the hydroranch at all as he calls it. He says he's embarrassed he doesn't want people to know he spent so much on the equipment. Everyone agrees he talks to them one by one but Paul suspects that after a few drinks someone will forget will take guests down into the basement on a tour. The hydroponics are a part of the basement so they'll be a part of the show. So what's he supposed to do. His plants aren't ready to be harvested pulled up hung to dry. Paul thinks he's made a mistake even mentioning the equipment

doing so's reminded everyone it's downstairs and probably his request seems suspicious it indicates he's probably doing what he promised he wouldn't. Grow dope that is when Paul thinks about it it seems that people are looking at him sideways.

THE CHILDREN OF FRANKENSTEIN

Al says that everyone at the party will be welcome upstairs if they're interested in checking out the livecam or maybe posing for a picture or two maybe or writing a few words for the The Children of Frankenstein's loyal viewers visitors fans. What loyal viewers Joan asks. What's there to be a fan of Joan asks. Al can't say at least not right now he's got to be somewhere.

The Children of Frankenstein

Al doesn't know if The Children of Frankenstein livecam has loyal viewers visitors fans. Plural. But Al knows that the Children of Frankenstein livecam has one fan singular and where there's one Al tells Paul in the evening in the attic there might be another. It's that only one fan's figured out how to get in touch figured out Al's username from the livecam website url plugged it into the U of F email directory and written. Is what Al figures happened is exactly what Al didn't want he didn't post his or anyone else's email address on the C of F website but it doesn't take a genius he tells Paul. He's sure Paul knows this to track an address down. Email or otherwise Paul says the U of

F directory lists email addresses and home addresses. Which is kind of creepy Paul scratches his nose doesn't know if he needs to say what they're both thinking then goes ahead because this guy knows where The Mansion is where we live. Yes he does Al says watching Paul and our visitor says that he's local though I don't know if I believe that. What I do believe Al says is that our friend is a guy just like he says his email always has a tone that Al recognizes. It's male not female it's a tone that he at least has never heard a woman take creepy voyeuristic pathetic. Well he tells Paul it was creepy voyeuristic pathetic when the emails first started coming when Al introduced everyone on the livecam when there was just the occasional picture flashed to the screen. The emails at that point asked questions the writer wanted to know everything there was to know about The Children he wanted details about the women especially but everyone in general. Who they were what they did who slept with whom what their lives were like then after a while he seemed to know these things or think he did. Which Al figures happened soon after he first posted his little paragraph about The Children. Meaning their fan's probably gotten some of what he thinks he knows from Paul. Al's seen some of the things that Paul's written on the webpage some of the pieces that Paul posted about life in The Mansion. But Al doesn't know how many of those pieces he's seen he's sure he hasn't seen them all he looks at Paul. Then his emails stopped being just creepy voyeuristic pathetic and they started being perverse hostile even violent is what Al says. Perverse Paul asks. Hostile. Violent. Al doesn't say anything he looks over Paul's head coughs. Perverse Paul asks. Hostile. Violent. He's got it in for Cloud Al says he thinks he's a twerp is how he puts it and he'd like to pound his head in he says. Ralph he thinks is a pompous ass a poser. Wind he's got disdain for though in a weird way the kind of disdain people have for their bosses. Evelyn Al says he seems to put up with because she's complex difficult. He can't meet Paul's eyes Feather he wants to beat up it's a power thing I think. Joan Al says he wants to fuck. And what about you Paul asks. Me Al says he thinks I'm curious. It's weird but he believes he's like me somehow

Al says but he's got that wrong. What about me Paul asks. You he likes Al says he doesn't say anything else. Wow Paul says shit. Weird. This guy seems to think The Children are real for real he seems a little overinvolved. Or maybe Al says he isn't maybe he's himself playing a part trying to yank our chains maybe he's making himself up as he goes along. Maybe Al says he just wants to freak us all out. This is why Al hasn't written him back who knows if he's for real. And why Al hasn't told anyone about the emails why scare everyone if there's nothing to be scared about. And Al hasn't contacted AOL administrators the guy's got an AOL email account because Al can't be sure what the deal is what he'd say. If he did contact them they wouldn't give out the guy's identity. Al's sure of that but if it were a case of hate mail they'd contact authorities. Only Al's not sure if there can be such a thing as hate mail against livecam characters they're not real people actually not exactly. They're fictions in a story in a way. He's looked for info on the guy in AOL webpages he hasn't found any. The guy he tells Paul calls himself Doc. Al says I'm thinking about getting a trial membership to AOL. To see if members have access to information about other members information that nonmembers can't get. I don't think they do Paul says but he doesn't know in the long run what he knows is that AOL users can have up to five aliases for one account and if they don't want to post a profile on any one of those aliases they don't have to. He's used AOL before. You might as well give it a try he says. Who knows you might find something. Paul doesn't ask to see Doc's emails Al doesn't offer to pass them along.

The Children of Frankenstein

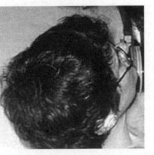

What Paul tells Joan is this he tells Joan that Al gets email from a faithful visitor to The Children of Frankenstein livecam. What Joan asks Paul is this she asks who what where why when. But first she asks how it's a statement as much as a question really Al doesn't put his our emails on the livecam. Then she asks when meaning how often how long has this guy been writing Al then who who is he. Where's he emailing from. Then she wants to know for Paul this is the kicker what's there to email about. She hasn't seen a thing he's posted not at least since his first bit. No one has is what he figures they're not even reading it right now not even this paragraph. Paul offers Joan vague answers to her questions he doesn't want to lie but how can he tell her the truth he's not sure what it is anyway. Why does she think he would. Who does she think he is. He's just a guy a good child of the middle class a graduate student trying to get some work done. He needs to get back to work.

THE CHILDREN OF FRANKENSTEIN

Joan's not happy with vague answers vague answers are nothing more than a form of lying. Evelyn's inclined to agree with Joan that if Paul's being vague then Paul's covering his ass their fan's probably a kook something's up. But Evelyn says who cares either way if Paul's been posting things on the internet if there is a fan. Either way what's the big deal. Most internet content where Evelyn's concerned is finally harmless useless etcetera and anyone who would harass someone online is probably a dork a dope who doesn't even have the nerve to hassle you face to face a gutless coward there's nothing to fear. Joan doesn't care is what she says to them all it's their first official household meeting official Paul supposes because for this meeting a date and time and place was agreed upon by everyone and everyone had to come and now they're in the living room perched on every available space and Joan's saying over and over again that she just doesn't care. She doesn't care first she doesn't care that Paul's probably written things about someone who seems to be her on the livecam. But if her photo's been on the livecam then people visiting the livecam think that that's her to them whether it's really her or not. But she doesn't care if she's been online if her picture's been on the livecam and one representation of her has been associated with another representation of her she doesn't even know if this is all true or wild speculation. She can't seem to get a straight answer out of Paul and no one else seems to know. Fine. She just doesn't care. That's the past. But on the other hand she doesn't care number two she doesn't care if Paul wants to keep doing what he may or may not have been doing why else would they have a fan why would some kook be emailing if there weren't something to email about but. Hold it. That's neither here nor there. The thing right now that Joan doesn't care number two is if Paul wants to keep doing what he may or may not have been doing. He cannot. He cannot keep on doing what he may or may not have been doing. This first and foremost where she's concerned. She doesn't want to be on the internet. Anymore at least assuming she once was. Okay. Have you checked to see if you were Wind wants to know. On the internet. If any of us were. For Joan this is beside the point meaning no. She doesn't like computers she doesn't know how she'd go about checking anyway she's forgotten the url it seems everyone has. Except probably Al and Paul. The point is that she does not want to be in any shape or form under any name she doesn't want to be visually textually in any incarnation on the internet. Capische. Okay. Paul keeps his mouth closed he knows when to shut up. He nods he stares he doesn't say word one. It's what Paul does when he doesn't want to won't can't engage he stonewalls. He can do this with AlWind FeatherRalphCloudandEvelyn they won't ask him anything directly. Like him they have a problem with straightforwardness. They don't want to be here any more than he does. He shrugs his shoulders it's all he offers. This makes everyone uncomfortable still no one says a word. What he thinks is fine and it is fine. He won't write another word about any of them. What he thinks is he'll write about Goose Branch Blossom Eucalyptus Dawn Hawk Lance and Sammy. That's not them is it. Not exactly. Too much is what Goose thinks this is just too fucking much. Sometimes he doesn't know when to stop. He doesn't like being yelled at.

But Goose knows two things Goose knows that his response to the problem in The Mansion is a petulant one. And Goose knows that changing people's names is not going to change anything where the livecam is concerned. If not everyone then at least Dawn will from here on out know their url will be watching their webpage like a Hawk if he posts something anything to The Children of Frankenstein homepage even if it's not about people named MattMattCamBudAugustMelRonorGillian or even people named PaulRalphFeatherEvelynWindCloudJoanorAl he's going to cause more trouble things are going to go to hell maybe Dawn will move out and if Dawn moves out so will Sammy and maybe other people too and Goose can't have the story of The Children of Frankenstein end this way. It's not finished and if it's not finished then there's no chance that he can finish. Graduate school that is he'll have to pack it all in and start a whole new chapter no pun intended. Really thinks Goose this is not funny this is very serious. There's a lot at stake here so. Fine. No more livecam he'll go back to writing the kind of novel he was writing in the first place. So. This is it. This is the novel.

Dawn's not herself anymore she hasn't been for a few days. At least this is how Goose feels she acts strange around him cautious watchful overly polite. She never seems to say what's on her mind. She pauses before every sentence thinking weighing her words is how Goose takes her behavior. It's worst when he asks her a question it can be the most innocuous inquiry something simple friendly how are you doing or whatcha been up to. For these she pauses shifts her weight from foot to foot pulls her hair back from her face watches him she's got smoky hazel eyes. Goose has begun to notice more than he ever did before and only after a few seconds sometimes even a half a minute does she answer. I'm fine thanks for asking. Not much really how about you watching him. It's creepy unsettling it makes Goose feel lonely.

What makes Goose feel lonelier is that it's not just Dawn it's everyone. They're all acting weird on the look-out watching themselves around him. In the kitchen Branch stops reading when Goose wanders in lowers his book back flat against the table Goose can't get a look at the spine. He's just curious about Branch's latest interests. That's all and when he asks Sammy how his work is going they're watching tv together a commercial's on what's he supposed to do sit in silence Sammy says oh you know then under his breath what sounds something like catsapandybangageleaky. What Goose says. Nothing. Sammy seems nervous afraid afraid of Goose. Goose's thought is no way. That's an unreasonable fear. Isn't it. Goose passes Lance and Eucalyptus on the stairs he's going up they're going down. They stop talking. They'd been having an animated conversation before Goose had heard them. They saw him then suddenly nothing nada zip they make room for him to pass single file hup two three four hey hey hi. Ho. Ho. Ho. Is this some sort of joke. Only Blossom shows him any concern she can't not she's always been in one way or another and always will be into a Big Mother trip indulgent but not obsessive letting things come and letting things go. She wants to

give everyone what they want. If only she could. She
gives Goose a big hug when no one else is around just a
hug she doesn't say anything she squeezes him pats him
on the back Goose thinks she smells good. She smells of
patchouli and cat.

      Pictures are out of the question if anyone catches him
taking photos there will be trouble. So Goose comes up
with devious ways of snapping shots. He keeps his digital
camera hidden in bags he shoots through open zippers
pretending he's searching for a book a notepad a pen. He
lurks in the oddest places and snaps off hip-shots before
anyone sees he's around. The pictures are just for him.
Weren't they always. In a sense. But how Goose wonders
is he supposed to write about people who won't let him
know what's happening in their lives. What's he to do
maybe let the rest of his book be the story of a Goose's
alienation no. He can eavesdrop he figures and he'll just
make stuff up. Which is what he's been doing all along
after all isn't it. He's an omniscient narrator but he's not an
omniscient person he can't really know what other people
think what they do behind closed doors. Can he. Has he.
Known. All he can do is extrapolate speculate about
people's inner lives and this after observing their words
their actions the clues they leave about themselves. He
puts together the pieces in a way that seems to see behind
doors making a believable mosaic out of fragments. Only
now he'll have to make more of less is what Goose thinks
more of less immediate clues and maybe it's for the best.
Somehow liberating is what Goose thinks. He can just
imagine the possibilities. He absolutely must in fact

because the show must go on. Is what they all think
they're going ahead with the party though no one seems
at all excited.

      Blossom's got a secret it's a secret she'd rather not
have it's the same old story. Blossom's missed her period.
Once is no big deal for Blossom it happens but twice.
Locked in the upstairs bathroom peeing on the white
testing stick she gets her hand wet she's never done this
before she's never had to. She doesn't have a facility for
targeted peeing but she gets the stick the strip soaked too
and after a few minutes it gives her a sign a color the
wrong sign the wrong color. Wrong for this point in her
life. Blossom's not ready to have a child. Blossom doesn't
have the time the energy the money the kind of relationship she thinks. To have a child. Blossom loves children.
Sometimes she thinks of Branch as a child there's something so boyish about him. She loves it when Branch is at
one then another of her nipples that's something else.
Really though it is. Something else. Not parenthood not
motherhood angry crying babies two year olds squeezing
glue into their mouths four year olds shouting arguing
breaking everything in sight. That's not all Blossom knows
but that's a lot a lot to deal with she's already got enough
to deal with. A baby means that she won't have time for
her work she won't be able to go out she'll be tired all the
time. She'll get fat. She'll get fat and Branch. Who knows if
Branch will be any help. Who knows if Branch will still
want her want to be with her. Who knows if Branch is
ready to be a parent. Maybe he thinks there are already
too many children in the world already so many they're

starving to death no one can feed them all. But a baby.
But a baby. It changes everything. Blossom wishes there
were someone she could talk to she thinks she might call
her mother even. She knows she can't. Blossom thinks
she'll get an abortion.

Sammy's got his blindspots there are things he
doesn't notice doesn't see there are reasons he can't. See.
Some things he can't won't handle so doesn't recognize
until maybe they slap him in the face. Like Dawn it's the
first time she's ever hit him she doesn't even like to yell.
Or get upset even now when he sees something's up what
it is he doesn't know. But neither does she she's just tense
unhappy scared she's sorry she's not sure what's going on
neither is Sammy. What he is sure of all of a sudden is
he's not trusted. He's not trusted by GooseBranchBlossom
EucalyptusHawkandLance. And Dawn. Not not trusted not
distrusted but not thought much of. He's not someone to
put faith in he can't be counted on he's not reliable. He's
not trustworthy. Maybe maybe not maybe he's making
things up speculating about his friends and Dawn in an
exaggerated paranoid way but. But Sammy's never been
hit before never that he can remember never punched
slapped whacked whatever. It's shaking a feeling out of
him and this feeling is that he's not trusted it's a sensation
that rolls around behind his eyeballs and travels down the
nerves of his arms to his fingertips which are twitching
and what he thinks of are chips. He's in charge of chips
for the party is all he's been given charge of and transportation of liquid refreshments those he's not even in charge
of he's just the wheel man. To Dawn he says I think I'm

going to spruce up The Mansion. For the party string
some decorations and hang them on the walls get some
balloons maybe a piñata. These are the only party decorations Sammy can think of the kinds of things he remembers from birthday parties when he was growing up. Or
something he says some kind of decorations I'm going to
liven things up.

What Dawn asks is what. What are you talking about.

Where it is Branch spends his days and half his
evenings no one knows not even Blossom. What they do
know is that it's not in The Mansion this is pretty obvious
to even Eucalyptus who herself hasn't been around the
house much or Hawk who's not often in The Mansion
proper. Branch leaves early early for him at eight or nine
and comes back late seven or so when he is in The
Mansion he's in his room. His and Blossom's room he tells
her he was on campus he tells her he was in his office or
the library. If they don't meet for dinner on campus or
downtown they eat in their room it's what Branch wants
he says to have a little privacy while they eat. It's weird is
what Blossom thinks and antisocial but on this Branch is
unmovable. He's in a groove he says he's getting things
done he's getting caught up on his work his teaching he's
even getting ahead. He doesn't want any distractions but
it's more than that. This is what Blossom suspects. What
she suspects further are several possibilities that fall under
her one larger notion that something's up. That something
she thinks is A maybe someone in The Mansion insulted
Branch he's very sensitive about being slighted. He's very
touchy. And A now he doesn't want to play with the other

kids which is pretty small behavior if that's what it is. Everyone gets slighted in one way or another you can't withdraw from humanity because it's filled with humans. This seems like a very plausible explanation of Branch's behavior. Only in Blossom's darker moods when she hasn't seen Branch all day long when it's late it's getting dark and she's hungry which she is more and more often lately she thinks it's B he's met someone else. Branch has met a student and he spends his days with her on campus at secret meetings in his office or off campus long afternoons of fucking at her place she's younger blond she's got enormous breasts it's not B it can't be B. She would know wouldn't she. When she thinks it's B she's letting her imagination run wild. This is the conclusion she usually reaches unless maybe it's C his affair is with someone in The Mansion and they both know her well enough that tricking her isn't such a challenge and they meet in his library carrel. When he says he's getting ahead that's a joke what he means to say is that he's getting a little head getting blowjobs in the library stacks. That's why C he can't stand to see anyone in The Mansion what if he sees her what if they can't hide it what if a glance slips and Blossom sees. What if someone else sees that glance or sees them together. That asshole. That bitch.

Eucalyptus can get tense tenser tensest without snapping she never flips out as she gets more nervous unhappy afraid angry she just gets tighter more wound. The snapping typically comes in the people around her first it was her family her sisters parents then friends in high school and college and after and now it's Lance.

They he put up with Eucalyptus's anguish and the vibe it
sends off as best they can for as long as they can. She's
not doing anything wrong after all just making everything
around her feel not quite right and then. When Lance
snaps it's in a big way he doesn't have enough imagination to do otherwise. He often has so little imagination
that he's completely at the mercy of what happens to him.
Lance is like a force of nature and a force of nature is
simply the product of every other force of nature and
while Eucalyptus in her frustrations is more than just a
force of nature she's still in part that. A force of nature and
when she becomes overwhelming she sets Lance in
motion and he's a rockslide. He's suddenly very able to
move in a straight line not worrying about a lot of
zigzaggy reasons for doing something or not doing something. When Lance snaps he doesn't think he does and
what Lance does is unpleasant. What does Lance do. He
throws the lamp against the bedroom wall it smashes into
pieces he punches the closet door until his fist is bleeding
he throws the telephone out the window he yells at
Eucalyptus tells her she's a miserable cunt the most
fucking depressing bitch on the fucking planet she's so
fucking joyless he could. Pack his clothes is what he does
pulling a duffel bag out of the closet pulling his clothes
out of the dresser drawers pulling the dresser drawers out
of the dresser and smashing them against the wall. What
he's going to do is move the fuck out of this fucking
dump he says I'm sick of you and I'm sick of every
fucking useless fuck in this place and he means it he's
only ever going to return to The Mansion to pick up the
rest of his stuff. He's going to find his own place. His own
fucking place.

Fine is what Eucalyptus says of this of Lance's explosion. She's not afraid it's a relief it's the kind of thing that
precipitates change which is what she wants but can't
somehow make happen. She can only channel it when it
occurs. Let's move out she says we'll move out after the

semester is over or next summer at the latest. We'll get our own place she says. She says I think we should get married.

    About some things Goose can be very sneaky. About other things he's not so good. Like Anny she's been coming over more often coming straight to his room they've been getting it on. This Goose is having a hard time hiding first off Anny's run into everyone in The Mansion one time or another. Not Blossom not Branch but everyone else coming into The Mansion or in the hallway or later on her way to the bathroom. Or going out. And the sex that Goose's got no control over it's him and Anny making all sorts of noises that he suspects float through the house. It's only him and Anny too which makes them that much more obvious. No one else in The Mansion seems to fuck anymore. From what Goose can tell. To cap it all off Anny comes to The Mansion late she stays at The Mansion late sometimes she falls asleep in his bed. Goose wonders what her husband thinks. When Goose thinks too long and hard about it especially late at night he gets hinky he starts hearing things in The Mansion noises he starts seeing things outlined against the black of his bedroom window. Shapes movements. What else Goose hasn't hidden well is his stash Anny's seen it she's seen the grow lamps too though they're not growing anything anymore. He harvested. The reason Anny has seen his stash is because it's hard to stash it's about five pounds worth. He's got a steamer trunk and he puts his weed in there. You put your weed in there. Ha ha it's not a laughing matter. It's a felony offense and he'd rather no one

know about it especially Anny. Goose doesn't think that
Anny is all that reliable she's probably not good at keeping secrets. More and more lately Goose feels like a goose
it has everything to do with the fact that he's sticking his
neck out.

     Hawk feels really bad when things get fucked up for
Hawk they feel very very very very fucked up. To him.
What he has little control over are his emotions it's why
he tries to keep them at a distance. But he's only human
after all and when things start to seem feel be bad for him
he becomes completely immersed in them he can't find a
way out. Of his emotions. Hawk needs to watch out
because he's gotten too attached to Karen and Karen's
leaving. Not right away but it's inevitable. She's applying
for jobs she's got interviews lined up for winter break
she's not going to be around the U of F much longer and
he is. Even when she's around next spring Hawk thinks
she won't be she'll start pulling away even before she
knows where she's going or if she's going for sure. Which
she will be. Hawk's got a gut feeling it's totally irrational
given the market but that's where Hawk knows what he
knows. He's been having terrible stomachaches lately
headaches too. Feeling bad about Karen's made him
vulnerable to feeling bad about The Mansion too and to
his mindbody there's plenty to feel bad about. There's
something very wrong in The Mansion and Hawk's idea is
that they have a group poltergeist. What this implies about
The Children isn't pleasant to think about. It implies
there's a lot of loose energy generated in the group it
implies that the form of their bond is no longer adequate

to contain its own energy. At the same time it implies an energy loss a hemorrhage. A loss of affect of feeling interest caring for each other there's been a deflation a flattening out. Except in Hawk he feels like he's ballooning with every uncontrolled molecule discharged by GooseBranchBlossomEucalyptusSammyandLance. What he starts saying to everyone when he sees them is When are we going to have this party.

A party the party. Fuck it. Branch can't stand the idea he doesn't have the time the inclination what's to celebrate anyway. Isn't the reason for having a party to celebrate something to share your happiness joy bounty with friends acquaintances the partygoers. Branch doesn't feel happiness joy he doesn't think anyone in The Mansion does. All they feel he thinks is ambivalence suspicion irritation even animosity. Branch isn't overly prone to superstition but he can't shake his feeling that every corner of The Mansion is filled with shadows. Wherever he turns in the kitchen the living room the hallways the bathrooms. Light from lamps or from outside isn't sufficient to illuminate corners crannies spaces under tables cabinets next to bookcases. God. What a joke they're living in a haunted house The Haunted Mansion of The Children of Frankenstein. Ridiculous. Branch can't stand to be there anymore he doesn't like to be home it doesn't feel right. There's some bad mojo about. Or something. Bjorsq. Blossom's keeping something from him when he's home she watches him but never says anything to him nothing substantial. He can't think of the last time they had a real conversation. He thinks he knows what's going on she's decided she doesn't love him anymore. Why he doesn't know. How can a person ever know about something like that. Fine. Bitch. Two can play that game.

From Lance there is animosity hostility irritation even anger. It's directed at no one in particular but everyone in The Mansion. What Lance thinks is there's a simple rule subtending all things and this is if you commit you follow through. If you say you're going to have a party you have a party you organize you act you do it. You do not dick around. You do not procrastinate. You do not change your mind. If you say you're going to have a party you have a fucking party. You have a fucking party even if you're so exhausted the likelihood that you'll enjoy said party is almost nil. That's how Lance feels. In every sense he's wiped out he's running on autopilot and the end of the semester is not in sight. Or. If it's in sight it's not within reach. Twice this week Lance had the same experience standing in front of his classes. Lecturing. He heard someone talking in the front of the room someone right next to him. Both times he turned his head and saw that it was him. Talking. To a group he saw when he turned his head again. They appeared to be listening to him. To which him. Whichever. Both times Lance paused. Neither time could he remember what day it was what semester what year. It didn't stop him from starting to talk again. About what. Whatever. Whatever it was it was probably the right thing to be talking about Lance is a very good teacher. It's what his students say it's what they write in their evaluations. He knows his stuff he's very organized he's very direct he's very clear. They know what he wants. They know what they have to do. Lance likes teaching.

This is how Blossom sees things. After some thought. If she's pregnant she has certain options after all it's the nineties. She can have the baby without Branch. She can take care of the baby on her own there are people places that will help at first her family her friends will help her get her strength back after the birth. They can help with feedings changing diapers. Then there are strangers there's day care at the campus. There are bound to be others who can provide day care too if she doesn't like the facilities on campus. All this will slow her down she'll make it through grad school more slowly. She won't get her dissertation done as fast as she wants but she won't have to quit school will she. She won't have to give up her TA will she. She won't have to run out and get a real job will she. No. Being in grad school might be the best thing for her for the baby it provides her with a flexible schedule. Yes. She can do this she can do this. Except for the money. She's not going to have enough money to take care of a baby day care costs money. She's not sure she likes the idea of day care anyway leaving her child with strangers letting them raise himher for half the day for half its waking life. Will it make a difference if it's a boy or a girl maybe boys can handle day care better than girls. Maybe it's the other way around she doesn't know she doesn't know if she wants a boy. She doesn't know if she wants a girl. Blossom thinks her parents will want a boy they never had a boy of their own. Blossom wonders what else her parents will want. They'll want to give her money they'll want to be involved they'll want to take care

of the baby when they can. Maybe they'll want her to
move in with them at least at first so they can help her
with the baby and in this help her continue in grad
school. This is what her mother will want her mother
wants her daughter to get a Ph.D. She wants her daughter
to be a capable career woman wants her daughter to
succeed in ways she did and ways she didn't. Maybe her
mother will want her to get an abortion. This is something
that Blossom hasn't considered before but it seems possible her parents are progressive they understand what
women sometimes have to do. They'll understand what
she might have to do. Sometimes people aren't ready to
become parents. Blossom wonders if they would if her
mother would ever actually suggest an abortion. She'll
know this is an option Blossom hasn't stopped considering it from when she first figured out she was pregnant.
She still considers it very seriously. Blossom's not sure she
wants a baby. Blossom doesn't know who she can talk to
about this and keep it a secret. She's not ready to talk to
Branch. Maybe Anny. Who could Anny tell.

Goose is in his room it's the safest place in the
house. It's the only place he can go to avoid the bad
mojo flooding The Mansion. The negative energy. The
negative energy in The Mansion is so thick that what.
Goose doesn't know exactly. He knows that it's thick
enough to cut with a knife as thick as pea soup but. He
doesn't like to think in clichés. When clichés are all that
are available he'd rather do without so he doesn't know
how to think of the mood in The Mansion. He knows it's
not good. That's not bad it's good in a way since Goose

has expected this all along problems tension anxiety unhappiness distrust etcetera. He's expected it expected everything. He's wanted it even this is how things are supposed to turn out for The Children. Says who says Sukenick. So if everything's falling apart then things are coming together. For Goose. It means he's got the idea. The Idea. But still he's upset that they're not having the party not managing to pull it together. It's a small thing a stupid problem but small stupid things have meaning too and if they can't have a party it's because they can't find anything to celebrate or to celebrate together. What a bummer is what Goose thinks.

On the other hand Goose thinks that everything has its seasons and The Children seem to be if not in at least headed for the dead of winter. Goose is watching reruns he's watching Friends. Which is almost too precious is what Goose thinks. If like him you don't have your own friends you can watch some on tv. Goose wonders if Friends can be good past five seasons. Probably not that's just the way things are the way things work out for shows the decent ones at least. There's the exhilarating if nervous start and then the blessed space where the actors figure out their characters the characters figure out each other and the writers are inspired by the flow. Then the comfortable sharp funny groove it lasts for a while. Then the moment when everyone's coasting out of ideas. The actors have outgrown their characters the show's outgrown its moment and it seems like it would be nice if things were over. Maybe it's best if everyone moves out. Sometimes you just have to know when to draw the curtain and move on. After all Goose doesn't want this moment to drag on for too long. A part of him doesn't want to let go of what he's what they've got had. He'll miss Eucalyptus LanceSammyBranchBlossomDawnandevenHawk when they're not around. But less than he thought he would. This is what he's begun to suspect.

What Dawn does every day before leaving The Mansion is make her bed. Her bed Sammy's bed. She pulls the sheets the blankets up she straightens them smooths them she fluffs the pillows places them next to each other against the headboard. She straightens their room makes sure the dirty clothes are in the hamper the piles of books and papers and magazines are organized. She hangs her towel on the closet door handle. Anything else that needs to be done she does. Then she cleans up whatever needs to be cleaned in the kitchen her mess and Sammy's. If there is a mess if there's something she missed the night before or made in the morning. Or that Sammy did. Then she straightens the living room. Whatever needs to be done she does and when she's done doing these things they don't need to be thought of again until the evening perhaps. Or the next morning. Of life in The Mansion of life in general right now Dawn thinks these things suck. So what. That's life. What are you going to do but muddle through. Maybe at one time she thought these things could be transcended but no. Maybe at one time she thought that life's painful difficult moments are something to be made of to feel deeply to learn from tap into that they are something deeper more profound more sublime. The whiff of real love or real death or real madness.

Maybe this is what everyone thought or thinks. This is what her parents thought what she suspects all The Children's parents thought. Maybe this is what her friends still think. But this is not what it's all about is how Dawn's begun to see it. What it's all about is plodding along. Sometimes you feel okay sometimes you feel like shit whatever. Whatever. Grow up. Dawn's been seeing a therapist. They've been working on helping Dawn get perspective. Dawn wishes Sammy would see a therapist too she can't handle his tendency to drag her down or rather off into his twitchfits. He's been worse than ever lately. He lies around the bedroom the living room half dead with quandariness. She can't handle her problems and his problems too so mostly she tries to not talk to Sammy. She doesn't want to know. She doesn't think a relationship can endure this kind of willed ignorance she's not sure she wants one that could. But she can't think about this just yet. What Dawn wants to know about is Hawk she's heard him late several nights in a row sobbing. This is what it sounds like through the ceiling. Sobbing. Dawn can't quite believe it she can't imagine that Hawk would ever sob Sammy never hears a thing. But stop hold it. If Hawk is sobbing she doesn't want to know. She does not want to know. That's it. Period.

Why tell anyone Eucalyptus asks it's not so much a question as a statement. Let's not tell anyone is what Eucalyptus is saying there's no point. Nothing has changed between them except theoretically except in a future sense. And it would be ridiculous is what she says to Lance to make a big fuss. I don't want to buy into all the ridiculous crap surrounding what is essentially a ridiculous institution. This is what she says. What she doesn't say Lance notices is Let's not get married. Eucalyptus does not say this she does not say Why bother. He thinks this is very interesting but he does not say as much. He doesn't ask But then why bother. He does not say anything. What does Lance know. Lance knows that he doesn't have to understand Eucalyptus to understand Eucalyptus. What doesn't Lance understand. Eucalyptus's reasons for bashing marriage or rather he understands her arguments but not why why she's making them. What does Lance understand. Lance understands that whatever she might say Eucalyptus really wants to get married. Her unspoken reasons for actually wanting to get married these Lance does not understand. He supposes that her reasons are the usual ones she wants a legal commitment she wants a ceremony celebrating it. She wants to be special for a day. She wants a set of china. Lance also understands that these are reasons Eucalyptus would deny if he asked her about them what else does Lance know. Lance knows that he would ruin everything if he pushed Eucalyptus into recognizing the ambivalence even hypocrisy in her position. He would certainly make life hard for himself. So Lance keeps his mouth shut. Why not. Lance wants to get married. He wants to have a life together he wants it to be taken seriously he wants for them to get their own place. He thinks he wants kids that's something he's not quite ready to think about seriously but. He wants he guesses to return to the kind of life he had before grad school something more stable normal etcetera. That's a part of it at least. He thinks. But he's still in grad school will be in grad school for a while. He's determined to get his degree. Eucalyptus has talked about dropping out. Why not the academic market seems hopeless. Why not get a real job. Again.

Though she expects it Blossom's still irritated when
Branch asks if she's sure. Of course she's sure. Of course
she's sure what a stupid fucking question. But then again
Blossom understands Branch is coming to this cold. He's
going to have all the initial reactions questions he's going
to be going through the things that she's already gone
through and come to terms with. Sort of come to terms
with. So okay. Yes she's sure she says she's known for a
while and there can be no doubt. To this Branch just
stares it scares Blossom. For a second only a second she
thinks she misunderstood him maybe he was asking
something else. Maybe he wants to know if she's sure it's
his. No. No fucking way Blossom's ears feel hot and red
but that's not it. No. Branch is just computing processing
trying to figure things out. What is Branch trying to figure
out. Whether he's happy or sad. What this means in terms
of their relationship in terms of his life. What this means to
grad school his dissertation it always comes back to that
for all of them. Almost all of them. It used to at least what
Branch says is What do you want to do. What does that
mean.

What do you mean Blossom asks. What do I want to
do or what do I want us to do or what should we do.

I don't know Branch says I mean I don't know what
to think.

.

I don't know how I feel Branch says.

.

I just mean I guess what do you want to do.

What Blossom wants to do is make a decision. She
wants Branch's help in making it but probably she thinks
she won't get it. She's not sure why she thinks this. She

hasn't given him a chance really. But still. She thinks she's right she alone is going to have make a decision the decision. So she does. She decides to make up her own mind.

Hawk's in his attic. Karen doesn't return his calls she doesn't come by. He knows why it's the way things are things have changed. That's all. But he doesn't feel rational about it he feels miserable. He feels rejected unloved unworthy lonely he feels like shit. He feels. He feels stoned. He is stoned which doesn't help pot makes him irrational and that's not what he needs right now his mind shooting off in directions that all come back to Karen images of her smiling of her dancing in front of the livecam. To the image of her legs rising up along the sides of his face open to him his eyes his mouth he needs to stop smoking so much dope. This is what he knows but he doesn't want to. He likes the feeling the distraction from himself even if it's not the best distraction even if it's actually a refraction a distortion of the world his vision of the world is cracked open. God he misses her. Where is Hawk getting the pot he's going into Goose's room when Goose isn't there he's dipping into Goose's stash. Why not. Why not it's not like Goose is going to miss it and Hawk wants it. Goose would give it to him anyway. All he'd have to do is ask but he doesn't want Goose on the one hand to know that he knows Goose has been growing dope in The Mansion. And on the other hand he doesn't want Goose to know he wantsneeds it he thinks Goose is pretty shrewd. Goose would know then what's up with Karen and Hawk's not ready to share how he feels. Though he thinks he might sometime soon he's going to stop sitting up in his attic at night with the lights out. Stoned. Watching out the window. It's fascinating what he sees when he stares out the window. For example Terry. Terry comes out of his house at least every other night weaves over to the remains of their garden and pisses on it. Hawk wonders if Terry pissed on their garden all summer he imagines Terry did. He wishes he'd known a little sooner. Well whatever. They wash their vegetables they washed them. Most of the time. Except when picking a tomato fresh off the vine and biting in. Hawk would rather not think about that. The other thing that Hawk does at night late is check the livecam it never changes anymore there's never anything on it but a picture of The Mansion it's what he put up after their house meeting. Instead of them The Children. But he checks it anyway he can't help himself some part of his mind expects it to change. He doesn't know why no one cares about it anymore. He doesn't get crank emails anymore he hasn't since the house meeting. But he checks it and checks it and flips to other sites on the web and comes back and checks it and tonight there's something. The picture's the same as usual but the text reads The Living Buddha is in town. The Living Buddha stops here on his journey from Tibet to Staten Island.

The Living Buddha is in exile an orphan of God. If The Dalai Lama dies then someone else The Living Buddha becomes The Dalai Lama.

When The Living Buddha dies someone else becomes the Living Buddha a small boy somewhere in the mountains of Tibet immediately becomes The Living Buddha. Then the priests have to find him. That's how they found The Living Buddha.

Someone goes to see The Living Buddha. A small brown man dressed in a white sheet greets him at the door. A small man with very big feet. He has the friendliest smile. He speaks no English. He grins. And he laughs.

Or sometimes he makes other sounds he grunts he growls
and as he makes the Yak dung tea he seems to click. Or
cluck. The Yak dung tea is the only thing he seems to
have of Tibet. Yak dung tea is not tea of dung but tea held
together in a brick by dung of Yak. This gives it a special
flavor. The Living Buddha seems to gaze at his visitor with
great curiosity brown eyes blazing with curiosity and good
humor. It's a curiosity that makes his visitor feel confused
and light. A curiosity he would like to oblige of which he
has no fear. He's not afraid. That alone is enough to make
him cry. He wants to speak but he has nothing to say and
The Living Buddha doesn't understand English. They drink
their tea and The Living Buddha makes sounds at him. He
grunts he clucks he giggles. He giggles like a demented
child. It's very disconcerting and at the same time very
funny. Finally he takes an orange and peels it clucking his
nonsense. Grinning he hands his visitor half the orange.
As he eats he starts throwing the pits at his visitor and
giggling he keeps throwing them till his visitor laughs too.
Then he starts making funny gestures with his hands. He
gestures giggles nods. Gestures giggles nods. Gestures
giggles nods till his visitor catches on and imitates the
position of his hands whereupon he throws himself
backward explosion of delight rocking back and forth
gusts of laughter for a minute it looks like he's about to do
a backward somersault. And that's not all after that he gets
up and teaches his visitor a little dance step a dance with
the same odd hand gestures both of them laughing so
hard the laughing turns to crying and then the crying turns
to laughing and back to crying till there's no difference
between the laughing and crying. The visitor laughs and
cries he laughs and cries till he's about to piss in his pants.
He pisses in his pants that just makes him laugh harder
sobs of laughter arpeggios of laughter rainbows of laughter
and he can feel his bowels loosening he's going to take a
shit then and there unstoppable it's so funny he's howling
shrieking blubbering he thinks he's going to puke.

What Goose does is accuse Anny of pilfering his stash. If she wanted some dope he says all she had to do was ask for some. What she says is go fuck yourself and it looks like this is what Goose will have to do. He's not going to be fucking Anny anymore. Oh well. What Goose sees in his bedroom when he clicks into the livecam it's the story of The Living Buddha. What Goose also sees is a picture of Hawk naked but for a sheet wrapped around himself. He's not small and brown Hawk isn't but he's got the sheet right. This cracks Goose up. Goose also cracks up over the look on Hawk's face. Deranged. Wacky. He can't tell what the look is supposed to be he can't tell if Hawk is laughing or crying. Beautiful. Perfect. This cracks him up even more he imagines for a second he can through two floors hear Hawk in his attic laughing crying whatever. Thing is he knows that's not possible. So what.

Palestine

Interruption. Discontinuity. Imperfection. It can't be helped. This very instant as I write as you read a hundred things. A hundred things to tangle with resolve ignore before you are together. Together for an instant and smash it's all gone still it's worth it. I feel. This composure grown out of ongoing decomposition. So far there are fifty-eight words in this composition. They're the same sixty-two as in the final section of Ron's book does that make one hundred twenty-four words. Maybe. Maybe not. I go to Televisrael where I am well received because one I have connections that is I'm hardwired. I'm plugged into the source. This means no interference and because two this novel is based on a novel that is based on The Mosaic Law the law of mosaics or how to deal with parts in the absence of wholes. So here I am. Go figure. Karen and Kate are here we're spending the afternoon in my apartment. Karen and Kate are friends when we meet we discuss what's been happening in our lives we exchange comments and ideas about each other what we've been doing what we're planning. We talk about people we know the school we've gone to neighborhood goings on. They give me advice I return the favor when we're together we agree that our trio is exceptional there's good mojo between us a certain sympatico many people have had a group of friends like this everything we say to one another makes sense our level of communal understanding is profound sublime. When one of us begins to speak. The others can finish his sentence. Or hers and this is what we often do. It's hard to not become euphoric when we meet to imagine that we're communicating in a way all but impossible elsewhere that physically spiritually we share a sympathetic understanding of things usually reserved for lovers making love and for only a few of those at that. Of course there's room for mistakes for misunderstanding there are three of us after all and when one has more than two there can be miscommunication. In the course of this afternoon I might from one room hear Kate say to Karen something that I misinterpret mishear mistake and perhaps I for a while act crazy because my perceptions are incorrect but. This never lasts. Problems we resolve always always within a short time no more than an hour and then we hug. We can't believe is what we say that things got so crazy. Right now what Kate and Karen say is that they like me a lot they think I'm on the right track on the whole and I take them at their word. I'd tell you more of what they have to say but that's enough for now it's time for lunch. In Televisrael there are places where the trees come down to the ocean and this is where I like to eat. There are beach cabanas where you can have a long leisurely meal cooled by the breezes coming in across the water. Despite the flat stretches of storm swept skies everywhere across the world Televisrael has perfect weather all year round it has to do with location. Location location location where there's bad weather that's where Televisrael isn't if that makes sense. Don't worry if it doesn't. Think about the fact that in Televisrael all people are beautiful they have nut-brown skin beautiful frames no fat great proportions. The men have wide shoulders and tight waists big arms and a little hair on their toned chests. The women are all thin they're generally small except for their enormous breasts they display them whenever they can firm legs asses both the men and women have gleaming white teeth and brilliant charming smiles. Their hair is never out of place. Being as beautiful as they are people like to display themselves they wear skimpy clothes bathing suits they spend a lot of time on the beach running jumping playing in the sand. After lunch I catch a digital caravan across the continent. The ride is virtually free almost instantaneous it's like being in two places at once here and there. Now I'm there. Boulder. The people in Boulder speak my language which is to say they sometimes don't make any sense. When I try to make sense back to them it comes out the same way we're communicating in a very unique way when we talk it sounds like schnotz vergimult bjorsq. We have long sympathetic conversations that often end in laughter and embraces.

Noi voh hunza schnecken.

Nacha. Vash znagel p'tooi.

Vass nichayim sliss bachti noss spissel jachachiss. Giggles. Slaps on the back. Pass the water pipe. The friend I most particularly want to see today is the novelist Ronald Sukenick. Whether Ronald Sukenick is actually a novelist is as many things about Ronald Sukenick not clear. He may be a philosopher but if so why write long arguments that seem to be fictions. Ronald Sukenick's explanations about this are not entirely clear because he speaks a very special brand of English it's sometimes hard to follow understatement of the year. One suspects Stevens some-where in the background but again this is not entirely clear. I swing into his driveway it's long winding and uphill. Ronald Sukenick comes out in worn corduroys a turtleneck over it a thick scuffed leather jacket he walks calmly casually. Saalem he says I return his greeting. We settle in his garden among murmuring hummingbirds. They hover around us flitting in the shade of cypress and palms on the stone table a jug of clear water it's made in the shape of a whale. You pour through the blowspout. Ronald Sukenick fills a glass of water for me I thank him I

say I'm surprised to see cypress and palms in Boulder he
says th're nt cyprs & plms th're oak & fir and so they are.
Wht'll we tlk abt 2day he asks I shrug and smile.

2day we ask y rite says Ronald Sukenick.

An important question I say.

Yiss Ronald says & an impt actvty it gets us alng hlps
us recr8 r lives. It hlps us in2 an hnst pstn a plc whr we cn
say smthng abt r own xperiencs whr we cn say smthng
directly.

Directly I say. Can one say anything directly.

Wll the challng & cnscious paradx is tht no matter
how hrd u try 2 gt dwn the literal data thr r almst no litrl
dta they r alwys filtrd throo the cr8ive mind. But u shld
alwys TRY to captr th dta of realit u have alwys 2 move in
the direction of th dta of xperince in reality whatvr th
chances u can't do this u have 2 try u have 2 try bcause it
is only in mking tht ef4t 2 deal with thse dta tht u finly
cre8 a legtmte fiction. U don't cre8 a legtmate fiction mrly
dealng wth othr fictions u need 2 get beynd them 2 get 2
wht lies beynd constrcts.

Which is I ask. To what is the matter.

Yiss. Wht is th mattr. Ths is th same questn as wht is
th spirit. But oppsite.

I see.

Yiss. Is mattr spirit or is spirit mattr whch do u think.
I'm not sure.

Or is the same. Yiss. Corpuscle or plasma. Or th bth.
Thnk of feelings & feelings. Thr is xprienc bynd lnguag.
Thr r thngs tht go on in th snsorium of th bdy tht r
prelnguistc & also postlnguistc & tht may or may nt gt into
th lnguag systm. Thr is a hole chain of ths feelings in ths
sns of wht u xprienc when smbdy touches u or kicks u. &
tht feeling regsters in varyng ways. 4 instnce it sms az if
peopl r amnesiacs abt pain once its ovr so I dn't no wht
form pain tks in th lnguag systm. Thr r prbably lts of thngs
tht u feel phscally tht dn't gt in2 th lnguag sytm. Thn thrs
tht othr sns of feeling flng emotion & thr is a gradation.

Tht is bdily feeling trns in2 emotions mst ezily. Mybe pain
& fear or pn trning in2 fr.
    And sex.
    Yiss in a way sex mst of all bcauz it is pleasurable &
desired. Th reasn sex is so pwrful is becauz it's whr
feeling trns in2 feelings more eazily. It hlps us get byond
formulated emtns back 2 an undeniabl source of emtn.
Ths may b th same sense we get in lnguag or ficshnl
forms whn u psh it 2 gt bynd yr conceptual control our
cultrl cntrl our conventional cntrl. Tht 4 exmpl is xprienc
byond lnguag as far as I am cncrnd.
    Y. Y bother.
    U mst bthr if y dn't u r jst 1 of th lving dead. Rite.
Write. Tht is th problem tht is the matter.
    I see. I think. I know that Ron wouldn't steer me
wrong in Televisrael all advisors are to be trusted they
have in mind the best interests of their friends students
advisees. If they make mistakes if they guide people
wrong again it's never intentional as with Karen and Kate
they're only human we can learn about them from their
mistakes and our own we can forgive we can forget we
can move on. On to the next episode. This is what I tell
my students. They like 98.6 they like Sukenick he's turned
them on on several levels. They're excited they want to
start talking. So do I I feel like I can finally say what I
need to it's going to click at last I open my mouth and
begin. He was born in 1932 middle-class background. He
was well educated he's a prolific writer short stories
novels creative nonfiction criticism theory and so on.
Many awards including a Guggenheim no small potatoes.
All the while though he's been a notorious outsider and
activist formally typographically linguistically daring a
boundary crosser he moves between the serious and
absurd the clean and obscene the emotional and theoretical between genres fiction poetry biography autobiography criticism. His stuff can be hard. That's not the right
word. Challenging. That's good he's a thinker a writer a

person who refuses to distinguish between art literature
writing and life imagination it's what's all about participat-
ing in the active (re)creation of the world. It. Everything.
He says that one cannot have control over that of which
one is a part. One cannot formulate it completely. One
can only participate more deeply in it.

What happens if you don't do that.

Then that's what's the matter. Get it. No. I'll explain
later. For now 98.6. In particular. It comes in three parts
they portray three landscapes worlds three geographical
moments they're all three the same and different they
can be both at once it's a matter of perspective. Here's
one. Perspective. F equals a creation gone wrong the
land of the living dead nuff said. C of F equals using the
imagination to find new forms worlds it's about hope but
no sense of the ultimate harshness of reality that everything ends in death. What if you have that sense but you
don't quit hoping trying anyway. Then you've got P it's
about pushing away F and expanding the hope of C of F
until you have a luminous orgasm. In P everything can
come together pun intended. For one brief shining
moment it'll end everything ends in failure you can't help
that. But you can try again then you can come again you
can come to Palestine. What if we all work toward it
what if we aren't afraid of failure what if we know that
when things end badly they're actually just changing
breaking open when that happens you have a new
beginning start again try again. Do it over again. But
differently this time and the next the next. Failure is no
longer failure. Instead it gives you multiples and that's
good it's the extraordinary which as near as we can tell is
The Answer to The Problem. The Answer is pyramids the
jungle air filled with butterflies is the possibility of magic
it's the Ancien Caja. It's grappling with something other
than that which is normally understood. The extraordinary is about remaining open to the unknown. Not much
of that in F. More of it but also naivete in C of F. A whole

lot of it in P do you see plus awareness of the risks. Of being so open.

Tom is medium tall he has a shock of light brown hair what Tom shouts is Yes Captain. O My Captain he's enraptured as he looks toward the front of the room it's what I've been waiting to hear. I love it when they shout this I leap onto my desk I look at them with admiration and respect and awe they look back at me with the same. On one woman's face a look of pure love adoration. It makes me crazy with excitement.

But what about death. This from Tom's friend he wears thick black glasses always looks like he's just woken up he's holding coffee. In *98.6* Sukenick seems so deadly serious so often death is always around the corner.

Well every wave crashes. That is the matter. But the spirit lives on maybe that's a statement maybe a question how do you know when I don't punctuate my sentences. Good question here's another one how should I know I'm not Ron Sukenick I'm Matt Roberson. Private. 065-26-6564.

True or false true or false. You're weirdly maybe even pathologically fascinated by Ronald Sukenick and or his work true or false you really think you are Ronald Sukenick true or false that's not your social security number it's his true or false true or false you're afraid to give your own.

Matt Roberson. Private. 065-26-6564.

It's a good question it's the one Cam asks he fixes me with his look a stare he doesn't expect me to answer not as if I know what I'm talking about. More as if I'm asking my own question in response he'll then ask another question about which I'll have a question to which he'll respond with an answer that sounds like a question that I'll answer etc. We tend to go on like this for hours. Cam introduced me to Sukenick. The man or the text. THERE'S NO DIFFERENCE.

You don't really believe there's no difference Cam says.

I do. I believe what I'm saying in this equation there are of course unacknowledged subtleties but on the other hand. I believe. I believe because I want to believe. Let me give you an example. One of Televisrael's most beloved figures is Cam Tatham he's six foot one or two thin he's got a distinguished head of graying hair an enormously full beard he often pulls strokes twirls. Cam has played many roles over the years what he is now is beloved husband and father. We all look up to him he works hard to make Lynn and the kids happy. He's wise understanding kind patient experienced. He never loses his temper ever he smokes a pipe Cam Tatham wears cardigans with elbow patches he's strict but not ungenerous never seen drinking he always emerges onto a scene just when he's needed never before. He never stays longer than he's needed he makes like Sukenick for a good advisor it's what he's been to me he's good at maintaining a continuous self vibrating region of intensities whose development avoids any orientation toward a culmination point or external end. That's the man. And the text. Only in it all there's an immense fear. These are all ravings I've got important practical things to do I've got to find a new place to live I've got to move I've got to figure out a new school I've got to get ready for the job market. I've got to get a tenure track job I've got to get this book finished I've got to pay off my car repairs. Car repairs don't exist in many parts of Televisrael there's no need for automobiles they have long been exiled from some cities and towns where transportation depends on various beasts of burden camels burros oxen. There are even a few llamas to be seen and modern experiments are underway with giraffes and zebras which in fact antedate the use of the horse in Africa and the Middle East. Many cities in Televisrael have extensive intercity monorail systems and colorful barges make their way among the canals. There are even starships believe it or not and teleportation devices you can dematerialize in one place one minute and rematerialize another place the next and in a flash you're halfway across the planet. But let's stay close to earth for the moment to the Holy Land where environmental planning is largely given over to artists with the result that Televisrael's native beauty has been preserved and even heightened. The prestige of novelists along with other artists is such that no intermediaries are needed between okay. What. What about sexuality Kate and Karen are troubled about it they want to know how we handle this matter in Televisrael not so much on a personal basis you understand but on the level of policy and metaphysics. I'm always glad to toss these things around with them but what particular aspect I ask do you have in mind.

We might begin with the question of loneliness.

Yes. That is at the heart of the matter as one might expect. Undeniably there is not one recorded instance where this did not have to be dealt with. Unless of course you eliminate feeling feeling of any kind and then you are well on the road to eliminating sexuality itself in fact we have developed an equation. L=C/L this is known as The Law of Insularity. Love equals communication divided by loneliness obviously a very unstable condition. Among its corollaries is that loneliness bears a positive relation to love the more love the more the potential loneliness. The only way to escape this consequence is to deny the fundamental importance of sexuality itself and drift off into philosophical abstractions an option today reserved for only the most puerile theorists. Add to the Law of Insularity the understanding that communication depends on one the fact of differing interests between any given love partners and two a basic conflict of interest between the sexes and we begin to see the dimensions of the problem. G of course comes to Televisrael with me we have been together many years and whatever fluctuations in our relation we've made all major moves together. Between us there is much love and there is much pain it is not a glib relation. According to the Law of Insularity the love is not constant it comes and goes in rhythms and waves that depend on communication. Which is divided by loneliness. Watching. In the midst of great waves of pain between G and myself fights threats mutual hysteria I find myself withdrawing I spend most of my days watching. What I am doing has been around since time immemorial you separate yourself from the world that is continue to walk and talk you interact when you must but most of the time your body moves on its own while you sit inside your forehead. What do you do you observe you wait. What are you waiting for you'll know it when you see it. Something other than what you have. What are you watching you like to watch people there are sophisticated ways of doing this at present there's no need to be around people to watch people. You can watch them on screens if you prefer real people on your screen they come to your computer. Now. From this doing nothing but watching and waiting comes the loneliness a fundamentally painful detachment. This loneliness can instead of driving you back to people estrange you farther it becomes a divide it divides you from what might be healthy communication if you a have a partner a wife the love is affected.

But why says Kate what do you hope to get Karen asks.

I'm not sure is what I say I can only say it's what you don't have. That is communication but also the never quite absence and the never quite presence of whom you watch and your desire to climb onto into around him or her or them. What happens next a certain flatness develops in regard to the viewed they become a parade of pixelated flesh where does one colored square begin and end where does the brown pixel meet the tan meet the blue. What else. Karen and Kate nod I know that they not only understand what I'm saying but that they know my words before I say them they've probably put these ideas into my head. It's as good an explanation as any for the origins of my theories. I don't know exactly where they come from.

Orgasm Karen.

As usual Karen's keyed in on the crucial question what needs to be asked. Orgasm is a lonely affair it's always had the potential to be lonely and it has often been so but now it is. More so. In a room lit by an underwater glow you press your hand against skin manipulating maneuvering what needs be maneuvered.

If.

If discharge is to take place. Prolonged human reception of electron streams has been proved to have a curiously stimulating effect on the human nervous system an overall quandariness is created in subjects as the body absorbs energy. This state of physical agitation can be relieved in any number of ways but mostly digits are manipulated around sensitive parts until in the case of the male a thin gruel spurts onto one hand. That's wiped off before the other turns again to finding a new vision that stimulates some need. This can be very sad this can bleed into all parts of the world.

But.

But don't get me wrong this is not all there is there are other options this is the good news. If you're aware of The Law of Insularity things become more interesting. Once you're aware of it you look at its components in a self-conscious manner things begin to change. Do you follow. A change in the field of consciousness is a change in the field of fact in one of the crucial factors in the field of fact. Such a change is known as Reversing Your Electrons. A reversed electron is a positron the physicists tell us that a positron may go backward in time. Yiss. If you reverse your electrons you find yourself in the Phase of Imagination where you understand you can always do more than watch you can act in your own dramas maybe you'll watch yourself doing so. They all the dramas begin with human connection it doesn't matter big or small flesh on flesh breath on flesh or flesh on breath. Or close geographic proximity of flesh to flesh what's important is that you feel the physical presence of others. This will result in biological manifestations they can be good or bad either way the fact of warming skin opening pores flared nostrils an itching down your back bumps on your arms these are all reactions they can't be ignored. And they are for good if human connection can be accompanied by interest trust positive waves of energy on your part mingling with those on the parts of others those around you then no kidding it's been proven your bones will tilt sideways your muscles will stretch and twist in a way that projects your belly button forward. You'll feel that site tingle when you're around those you trust the more you've needed wanted the more lonely you've been unlike what you are now the more the tingling. It can become a burning an ache it can be quite unsettling the only thing to do with such an itch is scratch it. The only way to scratch such an itch is to put your stomach against another's there's no amount of scraping with your own hands that will do this is where the sex comes in. No surprise there if you're rubbing your belly on someone else's you can do this through hugging through clothing but this never really calms the itch. You'll soon be rubbing your genitals it's just logical they're always after the tingling of the belly tingling themselves engorged with blood wanting the heat of friction the heat of warm wet tissue the vagina the mouth to excite and then draw off what then becomes unstoppable need. It's a need to go outward to push out to escape from yourself. These feelings come in ebbs and flows what can make them flow though without ebb at least for longer than most are aware is the accretion of energies of connection if you can draw together into one space a large number of people experiencing what we'll call The Phase of Imagination the waves of energy felt by all the connection tingling the belly itching the fucking sucking will be spurred on for all in a continually exponentially increasing manner the air will in fact pulse with a deep blue flare with some drips of

purple also some of red. It will seem to breathe on its
own without the use of human lungs in and out and in
and out and in its respiration generating a certain moist-
ness a smell of urgency. This is bound to create problems
The Phase of Imagination left unregulated uncontrolled
and spread through a group in a shared but ultimately
random manner will point in odd directions that are
inevitably incongruous by the simple fact that unfocused
energy will disperse in manifold directions if given the
chance. Pretty soon everything ruptures then everything is
shot to hell the energy released in this kind of spasming is
enormous ecstatic and terrible. A transmutation occurs not
unlike that in an atomic explosion the delicate balance of
personal and social forces is very much at risk if not
finally doomed. What can one do in such circumstances
but try to recompose himself herself withdraw to a corner
and refashion things according to not what has come
immediately before but by what came before that. Watching. Wariness. The Law of Insularity can be shifted into
The Phase of Imagination but it will always in some ways
remain constant present ready to reemerge. What can be
positive about the larger equation though is that the Law
of Insularity never applies in the same way to individuals
after The Phase of Imagination. There's always an alter-
ation for some this means the movement from no relation
to a relation of multiple to double for some the movement
from double to multiple to double in each case the double
being a new or newly conceived relation if this happens
and somehow the settling of patterns happens in a harmo-
nious way then the miraculous thing is that two people's
rhythms can coincide perfectly we can't know if this will
happen but if it does this is what we call love. Love is a
state that we can't know we can only experience it. But
the experience is a form of knowledge is it not. True it is
not abstract knowledge it is the initial form of knowledge
but perhaps it is also the final form of knowledge. I think
I've talked about this before though not in exactly this

way you decide. Partners in this new relation are in what's called The Phase of Illumination they will not go all the way with each other at first in sex you stop short of orgasm. When in this phase you neck a lot and play around you're like kids again. You use what is called The Rhythm Method in The Rhythm Method you try to sense your partner's rhythm you don't try to lay anything on him or her you get attuned. It's like a new combo tuning up if you don't get the rhythm you don't make the love. You wait. You come to the point of orgasm and then withdraw you withdraw back into yourself you contain the energy it fills you with a lot of energy the only trouble is it drives you crazy. All that energy instead of streaming out through your genitals detours into your head and presses against the top of your skull you feel like you're going to start levitating any minute if you don't fly off into the stratosphere at this point you become hyperconscious. You are now entering the state of Televisrael. In Televisrael the extraordinary is run-of-the-mill. In Televisrael people are capable of living in a state in which certain things that have happened have not. At the same time that they have. Do you see.

    I see Karen says says Kate. How long does your visit last.

    It depends it depends on an awareness and juggling of a virtually infinite number of variables interacting on a virtually infinite number of planes of existence. It will end in another failure of course and at the same time it's not at all a last chance. What we need to remember is that in it what's replaced is the teleology of should be and the retrospectiveness of if I had with who knows. Who knows what salvations we might pluck from circumstance if we are open to the unknown. Who knows. Bjorsq.

    This is utopia. No. It's madness.

    No. It's what I'm thinking as G and I celebrate moving to Televisrael we throw an enormous party in one corner of our banquet hall there's a jazz trio riffing jamming in another a bartender pouring drinks. It wouldn't be any fun for him if he couldn't have a few so that's okay he's a little drunk. The tables are covered in yellow tablecloths stiff starched linens sparkling silverware flatware glassware in the middle of each a bundle of flowers we've got friends in the catering business. They've set everything up they're here serving the guests they're taking care of us it's their pleasure. They say it makes them happy to make us happy we believe them they make it easy. We see them framed only occasionally as they move in between guests serving clearing they never do anything but smile working this party seems to be what they most want to be doing with their time. Patrick's in charge he yells when we don't keep things rolling drinks now food a little later dessert don't lag let people know when to get to the next thing. Lagging can ruin a gig. It wouldn't be Patrick if he didn't yell it's how he says he loves us. He's high strung temperamental but he's got a heart of gold. He's a real character. It all goes well everyone's here Andy Angela and Erik and Liana Cam's here and Lynn our families and Amy Dave Leslee and Pat and Elana old friends and new. Karen is here of course and Kate and Tom John Johanna Astrid and David Amelie and this is just the tip of the iceberg Carmen is here and Rachel Oric Kristie and Gwynne Andy and Patrice Mary is here and I can't even keep track everyone's a little loaded. We're all stuffed with food the band is doing Miles. I can't stop myself from hugging each person I see it's funny but G is doing the same when we see each other we smile we know what the other is thinking it's a happy moment. Everyone must feel exactly as we do there's no other way things could be. Andy and Angela are dancing by the door. We aren't on vacation in Televisrael we work. G works to organize events it's why we have so many friends in the catering business. There are a lot of events in Televisrael. People like to meet over meals it gives them a chance to communicate face to face. We have phones in Televisrael cell phones we have fax

machines email they're very useful and using them makes
their owners feel sophisticated but they're not favored
over face to face conversation in these people can see one
another's expressions touch each other's hands generate
physical communication. This is important around here it's
believed that while one can never reach the real meaning
behind another's words one should always try to move in
the direction of understanding the ideas in another's mind.
It is only in the effort to deal with these ideas that you can
come to know another person. It is only in coming to
know another person that you come to know about the
world around you. It is only in coming to know the world
around that you can create an honest position a place
where we can say something about our own experiences
where we can say something directly. Or as directly as we
can. This being the case G is in great demand she's paid
good money she's got social capital. She's what's known
as a discourse facilitator. She's quite good at what she
does it's a good thing there's always another job to work.
People in Televisrael have an inordinate amount of free
time in which to meet over meals. I work too I'm writing a
book. The book is a study of life in what might be the
contemporary world. It's equal parts analysis of my life
and analysis of my friends' lives. It's an analysis of my
friend Ron Sukenick's life too as he's experienced it
imagined it in the books I've read about not now but then.
Then. When. What. What's the difference between now
and then. That's a good question a big one in the book
which my friend the porfessor says is full of traces offering
up the presence of what's come before and finds a way to
simultaneously present lines of flight that illuminate
possibilities for future movement. This by allowing reso-
nances of levels that we've left to sound through levels
where we we might pick up some sense of what comes
next. And beyond. Sounds a lot like bullshit but something
can be made of it the book's general perversity perpetu-
ally striving for multiple threads and multiple directions all

working AT THE SAME TIME. Multiple threads reminding us of what Delouse and Guitar put a positive spin on as rhizomatics. As a schizoanalysis the book reveals layer upon layer a genuine multiplicity in which characters for example elide into extensions each with new names that parallel that similar strategy in a book that has come before in this case in Ron's book. What does that mean not what how. Energies of implication emerge as all levels link and link to a past which is a resonating backdrop constantly present and of course absent writing is an assemblage that is always collective that brings into play within us and outside us populations multiplicities territories becomings effects events. It's mimicry justifiably indulged such imitation properly executed brings along with it an intuitive comprehension of the ideas attitudes and modes of feeling that produced the style of expression at hand. What else as you've probably guessed the book's of course an analysis of its own analysis etc. It has a happy ending would you expect anything less everything finally works out the girl gets the boy the boy gets the girl the underdog wins the championship the hero gains self knowledge makes a journey through death and rebirth has a spiritual conversion. The bad person turns out good reformed. The mentor figure enables it all. The misfits get stepped on by an evil thug they turn around they get the thug back friends family lovers resolve their differences they're better than when they started. To fight. Everything gets back to normal everybody is free to go on with their lives as if nothing has happened the truth is out the mystery solved. Misunderstandings are made right parent and child are reunited. Someone is rescued. From what. From danger from him or herself from boredom the vampires are slain.

Still I have questions I WANT TO KNOW WHAT'S GOING ON IN THE DESERT SANDS OF NEW MEXICO. WHAT DID THEY REALLY FIND IN ROSWELL IT WASN'T A WEATHER BALLOON. WHY DON'T THEY RELEASE

THE REAL INFORMATION ON FLYING SAUCERS. WHY
DON'T THEY TRACK DOWN THE SASQUATCH. THE
ABOMINABLE SNOWMAN. WHY DON'T THEY TELL US
THE TRUTH. A RADIO BROADCAST IN TEXAS WAS
SUDDENLY RECEIVED FIVE YEARS LATER BY RESI-
DENTS OF LONDON. THREE-LEGGED ALBINOS HAVE
BEEN SEEN HOPPING AROUND IN THE MIDWEST.
MEAT RAINS FROM THE SKY. AN EXTRATERRESTRIAL
SATELLITE HAS BEEN DETECTED CIRCLING THE EARTH.
STARS ARE ARRANGED IN SEMAPHORE MESSAGES.

There are other questions we deal with in
Televisrael many have to do with negation we'd be fools
not to recognize its existence. Negation. After all there's
everything that's been lost we can't not notice what we
no longer have in this century alone six million Jews
thanks to Hitler. Two million Armenians thanks to the
Turks. A half a million a million Vietnamese thanks to the
French the Americans another several million people
generally to starvation and disease thanks to nature. But
also to worldwide apathy these are the big losses there
are also the small ones they're in some ways as significant. A plane has gone down over the Atlantic kids are
shooting up schools in the Midwest a flood takes any
number of lives. What we have is a host of disasters we
contemplate them all day long in one way or another we
hear about them from some head talking they remind us
of the possibility of our own loss of safety security
happiness they remind us that someone somewhere is
pissing on someone else's food. The attitude we take in
Televisrael is that these losses must be recognized we
have to think about everything that's been lost we have
to think about everyone who's died we have to think
about every tortured child woman raped man beaten
within an inch of his life. Why. Perhaps we want to be
prepared intellectually emotionally physically we want to
know what's going on. We want to be as hard as hard as
whatever it is that might hurt us. Perhaps perhaps though

this hardness is not always our goal in our better moments we recognize that you can't negate negation. You can't hurt horror any more than you can forget it you can't forget horrors as if they've never happened what do we get from remembering. Perhaps we learn to deny nothing in doing so we make the first step in incorporating the negation in the affirmation. This is us at our best we understand that when the negative is developed it becomes the positive like with the mass murders in our schools they've led after all to the outlawing of handguns for one but two better communication between parents and children mandatory classes in how to achieve this for all family members the sudden attention of our nation on public education the result being a massive influx of money for teachers books resources of all kinds do you see what I mean.

A reporter comes to see me he brings me a case of dyspepsia the official product of his corporate sponsor. He asks is it not true is it not that your generation is less ambitious less resourceful less moral less creative less intelligent less effective less committed and less likable than all other generations before it.

Are you kidding me.

Okay then it is true is it not that your generation is more spoiled more apathetic more self indulgent more selfish more impatient more wealthy more obtuse more unhappy and more likely than not than all other generations before it.

I don't follow.

You are are you not a representative of your generation.

Who exactly are you.

I'm the American who wants to know about the quality of life in The State of Televisrael. How many suicides do you have among males between the ages of twenty and thirty.

I don't know.

What percentage of the population votes in major elections.

I don't know.

What is the current rate of exchange between dollars and shekels. Between shekels and gold.

I don't know. I don't know.

How many members in your average mean family.

Our families aren't mean.

Don't kid around. What is your gross national product.

It's not gross.

Cooperate.

Do you want the quality of life or the quantity of life.

We want yardsticks. Most people in The State of Televisrael feel good when they get up in the morning. Yes or no.

Well it's hard to say a lot of it depends on dreams and the weather also the time of month probably a lot of people I know have told me they have certain physical rhythms that are relevant personally for me it's partly a question of whether I've made love the night before however I don't think you should feel bad about feeling bad when you wake up. That just makes you feel worse whereas these things tend to unkink themselves if left alone the other day for example when I got up my left ear was twitching.

No examples. Yes or no. People in your State breathe deeply and chew their food in a relaxed manner. Yes or no.

Well that depends on several things.

Yes or no yes or no. Most people in your State are content to sit on their porches in the evening. True or false.

I don't know I don't know I don't know I go to the doctor I hope for a diagnosis. What he looks like whether or not he wears glasses or has a beard I simply can't remember but this I know. He reminds me of somebody. I don't know exactly who I realize that he might not really be a doctor that he's just playing one for my sake. While I'm with him he rambles in a monologue punctuated by an intermittent static of nonsense. As he talks I find crazy things going through my head my eyeballs start to twitch. His thought processes are too fast I can't follow exactly what he says I catch one out of every three specifics I think I get the general drift the rest is over my head. This is on the one hand exciting being caught up in something bigger than me I feel outside my own body watching us talking or rather the doctor talking to me I get it I think I get things that is that I'd never considered before. On the other hand I'm terrified he's moving too fast for me I'm in a state of hyperattentiveness all my muscles are clenched sphincter to mind are rigid I'm trying to pull myself up to speed I want the right kind of focus to help me understand. This is what he says I am a terminal case. We all are. Whether this is bad the answer is yes and no. Whether this is good the same. Yes and no. He says that from the standpoint of consistency matters of expression must be considered not only in relation to their aptitude to form motifs and counterpoints but also in relation to the inhibitors and releasers that act on them and the mechanisms of innateness or learning heredity or acquisition that modulate them. Ethology's mistake is to restrict itself to a binary distribution of these factors even and especially when it is thought necessary to take both into account simultaneously to intermix them at every level of a tree of behaviors. Instead what should be done is to start from a positive notion capable of accounting for the very particular character the innate and the acquired assume in the rhizome and which is like the principle of their mixture. Such a notion cannot be arrived at in terms of behavior but rather only in terms of assemblage. He looks at me the doctor I haven't the first idea what he's thinking as he does I don't know what he sees when he sees me maybe he doesn't really see me at all. What does it mean to see a person anyway I don't think I often see myself well even

when I'm outside of my body staring back at myself I just
don't know. But while I consider this considering also
what the doctor has had to say I realize I've forgotten
everything else I've been troubling over. My mind has
flown in a line from its previous occupations I'm onto
something something else. Yes. I would like to hug the
doctor I think he would want me to maybe but I'm not
sure actually I think he would strike me down if I came
too close. Instead I think I'll pat his little dog a furry
handsome looking fellow tan with white paws I hadn't
noticed him before he leaps yipping onto his owner's lap.
I do nothing that will complicate matters further not right
now G strokes my back calming me down. I've been
screaming I've been screaming to her at her yes and no.
I'm a little worked up I can't quite catch my breath it's
okay it's okay it's okay okay it's okay G says and it is
really it's what I've been afraid of yes but it's exactly what
I've been looking for in a way it's the Holy Land and I
have faith from here on. I know that with G's help I'll
continue there's nothing we can't manage if we work
together. Toward common goals G and I can make extraordinary efforts we develop an unspoken appreciation
for the goals of obstacles to value in anything we undertake we know exactly what the other is thinking what
difficulties the other will face. All this without a word
spoken when we speak it's always about something worth
discussing and nothing else. We're after a successful
conclusion even though we fully appreciate the value the
meaningfulness of being in the middle of something. We
know though that you can't be in the middle of one thing
for your entire life. You have to move on maybe this
means failing at what you're doing this allows you to
leave where you are now. That means a successful conclusion is about the start of something different. What happens next we decide to have children. But not just yet.
First I meet Erik at his place. We ready his boat we're
going fishing. It's a perfect day the sun is shining but not

too hot the sky is a light blue there are no clouds. At the lake there are small waves this will be pleasant calm comfortable. We don't care if we catch fish. We'll enjoy being outside. This is not to say that we don't want to catch fish. Erik does. He's hopeful about the prospect he's hopeful about everything he does I point this out to him. He laughs says it's probably the result of stupidity the hopefulness. If he gave more thought to life he'd give up I know that he's kidding that with him the story is completely the opposite. Erik never stops giving thought to life he knows that this is the only way to make real the waves of his inner necessity. If he can allow in other words for his inner necessities then they stand a chance of being realized there's a chance they will coincide with the waves of outer necessity and when that happens another world is psychosynthesized when this happens you have what a friend of mine has called a Moment of Luminous Coincidence. The State of Televisrael is a Moment of Luminous Coincidence. Without the state of Televisrael life would become inconceivable it would lose a necessary dimension it would become flat we would each be on his or her own lonely and afraid. Erik has become actually quite an excellent fisherman his boat is so much nicer than I remember it's an enormous glistening woodhulled beast with purring engines we've got lines strung out at every possible angle there's absolutely no doubt as a matter of fact as I look at Erik and he looks back at me that we're going to catch a whopper the biggest fish we've either of us ever seen in our lives. It's an exciting moment and then one of the lines starts to sing. And then I start to sing the words are these you are perfectly right. Only experience can restore that lost synthesis which analysis has forced us to shatter. Experience alone can decide on truth. And while we're waiting faith. Faith enough to forge an art of experience to deal with our fate. You have to become an illogical positivist. In the state of Televisrael you become an illogical positivist. Yeah. Yeah. Yeah. Why not. At least

while you're in different stages of being in between
because on either end there's not variation it seems to me
that everything starts the same way everything ends the
same way. You can see it that way you do see don't you
think about origins. They must be back there somewhere.
Right. Ron. EVERYBODY PAUSE PLEASE GO TO YOUR
COMPUTERS BACK UP YOUR IMPORTANT DATA. SERI-
OUSLY. WHAT IF YOUR MACHINE CRASHES YOU'LL
LOSE DATA YOU'LL HAVE TO GO BACK RETRACE YOUR
STEPS DO EVERYTHING OVER AGAIN. WHILE YOU'RE
AT IT WRITE ME AN EMAIL. matthewr@uwm.edu. LET ME
KNOW WHAT YOU THINK. Can time run backwards that
is the question for today. The physicists say it is not
impossible. There are black holes in space antimatter time
reversed electrons. Maybe everything is happening at once
what then. One vast coincidence. Reread the last eighteen
lines it's very important. Rewrite them if you feel the urge.
Why not why not make this book your own our dreams
do no good unless we find ways of incorporating them
into our experience. Only experience can restore that lost
synthesis which analysis has forced us to shatter. Experience alone can decide on truth. An art of experience will
help us deal with our fate.

   And love.
   And love.
   And what you feel.
   And what you feel.
   And what do you feel.
   I feel that my dreams work according to the principle
of simultaneous multiplicity or the knack of keeping
several things on your mind at once. That is the central
fact of our mental atmosphere. That is the water in which
we swim or should I say the stew in which we cook. What
we have to become is master jugglers perfect a balancing
act. We have to become artists in the sense that circus
performers are called artists equilibrists who can do seven
things at once without thinking about it because we've

already thought about it. Or because our sages have
already thought about it thought it all out and we've
learned it from them. Make it look easy show us the easy
way easier and easier. Does that help. Yes. Yes it does.
Thank you. I think. Which is different from knowing. I
guess. Which is different from thinking is it. What I guess
I'm doing is stoking maybe stroking myself up to A Moment
of Luminous Coincidence. But it's not really a guess I guess
I don't have any choice do I not at this point. It's how this
all ends but that's a reductive way of looking at things
sure this is a little orchestrated but. But this is nothing if
not a constructivist enterprise. Desire is not a state of
nature. It exists only when assembled or machined. You
cannot grasp or conceive of a desire outside a determinate
assemblage on a plane which is not preexistent but which
must itself be constructed. Every assemblage expresses
and creates a desire by constructing the plane which
makes it possible and by making it possible brings it
about. Maybe when viewed from a rational perspective
this is confusing maybe ridiculous it confuses cause with
effect the objective with the method. So fuck rationalism
it's like this. Energy desire the plane of immanence constructed assemblages they're all immanent to one another
manifested differently only as relations on a stage of
activity. Desire is not a thing but a process of experimentation which by setting itself in motion establishes its
existence and its existence is the condition of its fulfill-
ment.

So.
So sometimes words fail us.
.
.
.
.
.
.

258

.

.

.

.

.

.

.

So you don't have to understand everything you remember. You have to love you have to feel.

S

E

W.

I will. I'm walkin with ma baby along the western shore of Lake Michigan I'm watching some tube I'm about to have a moment of Luminous Coincidence. I feel it coming on it's coming together IT'SNOTJESSELONECAT FULLERWHOSPENTHISLIFERAMBLINGBETWEENGEORGIA TEXASANDCALIFORNIAWHEREHEEVENTUALLYSETTLEDWHO ALONGTHEWAYLEARNEDSPIRITUALSBLUESRAGSANDHILL BILLYSONGSHEADAPTEDTHEMALLTOHISTWELVESTRING GUITARSTYLEBUTITWASNOTUNTIL1950THATHEDECIDED TOSEEKOUTWORKASAMUSICIANHEENCOUNTEREDTROUBLE FINDINGRELIABLESIDEMENSOHEBECAMEAONEMANBAND playing all the instruments ATTHESAMETIMEIT'SACTUALLY BUGSBUNNYHE'STHECULTURALICONOFMYTIMEANDIMEAN NODISPRESPECTBUTIT'SBUGSISEEWHENISEEANYONEAS AONEMANBANDOOMPHINGALONGWITHBANJOTROMBONE DRUMETCETERAHE'SMYGENERATIONSJESSELONECATTHE IDEASTHESAMETHEREHEISAFLOPPYEAREDHERO playing all the instruments AT THE SAME TIME I'm sitting in Milwaukee in my living room I'm watching cartoons on tv AT THE SAME TIME trying to finish my novel AT THE SAME TIME trying to forget it but on comes Gilligan's Island AT THE SAME TIME connecting to the internet I've got emails from writers contributing to my book on

Ronald Sukenick AT THE SAME TIME thinking about the
fact that Sukenick is a Mosaic Man a stitched bundle of
fragments AT THE SAME TIME worrying that there's no
difference between Frankenstein and a mosaic they're
both stitched bundles of fragments AT THE SAME TIME
not worrying they can be all at once the same and very
different beasts and I realize anyway that neither of them
is the be all end all I wouldn't want them to be AT THE
SAME TIME I'm thinking about dinner on Thursday with
Cam and Lynn my family away from my family AT THE
SAME TIME moving to Atlanta AT THE SAME TIME sorry
to leave Milwaukee AT THE SAME TIME AT THE SAME
TIME thinking about my friend Gareth who's been ill he's
had surgery he's told another friend that since he doesn't
have hair to cover the scars on his head he looks like
Frankenstein AT THE SAME TIME saying out loud the
words Gods and Monsters wondering about the role of
sexuality in The State of Televisrael AT THE SAME TIME
entering into The State of Televisrael AT THE SAME TIME
orchestrating the whole thing toward those Moments of
Luminous Coincidence when everything comes together
AT THE SAME TIME printing out a chunk of this book for
my writing group AT THE SAME TIME tying the damn
thing up AT THE SAME TIME happy to be heading to
Atlanta another chance AT THE SAME TIME my life is
unraveling AT THE SAME TIME this novel is bungled
fragments of bungled fragments stitched together AT THE
SAME TIME everything is seamless perfect not because
because because but AT THE SAME TIME having my
doubts letting it go as it is. Another failure.